THE SAVAGES

SCREENPLAY AND INTRODUCTION BY
TAMARA JENKINS

A Newmarket Shooting Script® Series Book

NEWMARKET PRESS • NEW YORK

FIRST EDITION

10   9   8   7   6   5   4   3   2   1

ISBN: 978-1-55704-800-4

Library of Congress Catalog-in-Publication Data available upon request.

QUANTITY PURCHASES

Companies, professional groups, clubs, and other organizations may qualify for special terms when ordering quantities
of this title. For information, write to Special Sales, Newmarket Press, 18 East 48th Street, New York, NY 10017;
call (212) 832-3575 or 1-800-669-3903; FAX (212) 832-3629; or e-mail info@newmarketpress.com.

Website: www.newmarketpress.com

Manufactured in the United States of America.

OTHER BOOKS IN THE NEWMARKET SHOOTING SCRIPT® SERIES INCLUDE:

About a Boy: The Shooting Script	*The Ice Storm: The Shooting Script*
Adaptation: The Shooting Script	*Little Miss Sunshine: The Shooting Script*
The Age of Innocence: The Shooting Script	*Margot at the Wedding: The Shooting Script*
American Beauty: The Shooting Script	*The Matrix: The Shooting Script*
A Beautiful Mind: The Shooting Script	*Michael Clayton: The Shooting Script*
The Birdcage: The Shooting Script	*The People vs. Larry Flynt: The Shooting Script*
Black Hawk Down: The Shooting Script	*Pieces of April: The Shooting Script*
Capote: The Shooting Script	*Punch-Drunk Love: The Shooting Script*
Cinderella Man: The Shooting Script	*Red Dragon: The Shooting Script*
The Constant Gardener: The Shooting Script	*The Shawshank Redemption: The Shooting Script*
Dan in Real Life: The Shooting Script	*Sideways: The Shooting Script*
Dead Man Walking: The Shooting Script	*Snow Falling on Cedars: The Shooting Script*
Eternal Sunshine of the Spotless Mind:	*The Squid and the Whale: The Shooting Script*
The Shooting Script	*State and Main: The Shooting Script*
Gods and Monsters: The Shooting Script	*Stranger Than Fiction: The Shooting Script*
Gosford Park: The Shooting Script	*Traffic: The Shooting Script*
Human Nature: The Shooting Script	*Transamerica: The Shooting Script*
Juno: The Shooting Script	*The Truman Show: The Shooting Script*
Knocked Up: The Shooting Script	*War of the Worlds: The Shooting Script*

OTHER NEWMARKET PICTORIAL MOVIEBOOKS AND NEWMARKET INSIDER FILM BOOKS INCLUDE:

*The Art of The Matrix**	*Hotel Rwanda: Bringing the True Story of an African Hero to Film**
*The Art of X2**	*The Kite Runner: A Portrait of the Marc Forster Film**
The Art of X-Men: The Last Stand	*The Jaws Log*
*Bram Stoker's Dracula: The Film and the Legend**	*Memoirs of a Geisha: A Portrait of the Film*
*Chicago: The Movie and Lyrics**	*Ray: A Tribute to the Movie, the Music, and the Man**
*Dances with Wolves: The Illustrated Story of the Epic Film**	*Rush Hour: Lights, Camera, Action*
Dreamgirls	*Saving Private Ryan: The Men, The Mission, The Movie*
*E.T. The Extra-Terrestrial: From Concept to Classic**	*Schindler's List: Images of the Steven Spielberg Film*
Gladiator: The Making of the Ridley Scott Epic Film	*Superbad: The Illustrated Moviebook**
Good Night, and Good Luck: The Screenplay and History Behind	*Tim Burton's Corpse Bride: An Invitation to the Wedding*
*the Landmark Movie**	

*Includes Screenplay

CONTENTS

INTRODUCTION

BY TAMARA JENKINS

There they were—Laura Linney, Philip Seymour Hoffman, and Philip Bosco in my living room—and I was feeling queasy. They were holding screenplays in their hands—my screenplay—that I wrote only a few feet away from the spot they were standing. I was in the kitchen making them coffee. I was steaming milk and arranging muffins on a plate. I wondered, "Did John Huston ever arrange muffins for his actors? Did Peckinpah steam milk?"

I was worried about the coffee, the screenplay, and my ability to direct a roomful of frighteningly talented actors. I hadn't made a movie in eight years. What had I been doing all that time? I got lost for a couple of years. I pursued jobs that went nowhere. I spent two years writing a screenplay that didn't get made. I met with executives on projects that never happened. I did good things, too. I directed theater. I made a short film that was written by teenagers. I acted in tiny parts in a couple of movies. I married a screenwriter. I performed in storytelling events. I did a rewrite job with my husband. I got a dog. Mostly, though, I wrote things: journal entries, essays, stories, random scenes, and finally this screenplay.

As I carried the coffee and muffins into the living room, it occurred to me that just a few months earlier I had been completely convinced that the movie was never going to happen at all. I certainly never would have imagined that I'd be sipping coffee and eating baked goods with three amazing actors as we embarked on our first rehearsal.

Flashback to November 2005. The screenplay for *The Savages* had been finished for over a year. The actors were attached, but we couldn't get the film off the ground. Despite the prodigious efforts of my producers, all the financiers were passing. No one wanted to make the movie and I was miserable.

On one particularly grim day, I got an encouraging e-mail from a friend pointing out that the Internet Movie Database had selected my first film, *Slums of Beverly Hills,* as their "Movie of the Day." I clicked on the link and, lo and behold, there was a bright color image of the poster from the film and an accompanying article that contained a lively plot summary and a few kind words. At the end of the article there was a biographical bit that attempted to explain what I had been doing during the eight years since my first feature. It said:

> Interestingly, Ms. Jenkins fled Hollywood after *Slums,* though she took small roles in a couple of films. She focused her attention on training to become an Olympic kayaker, and participated in her first Olympic games in Sydney in 2000.

If you Google "Tamara Jenkins," you might come across some pictures of a very tall, gorgeous blonde athlete described by *Esquire* as one of "The Sexy Women of Sports." For the record, I am not that Tamara Jenkins. I am not tall or blonde and I've never been anywhere near a kayak—although I have on two occasions canoed in Central Park.

While the other Tamara was training fiercely, I was sitting in my office—a spare bedroom in my apartment in the East Village of New York City—looking out the window and thinking about the nursing home on the corner of my block. I was scrawling notes in Cambridge legal pads and typing on my iMac. I was excavating aspects of my own life and freely fictionalizing as I saw fit.

The only exercise I was getting involved my dog, Weegee. He is a Jack Russell Terrier and needs lots of activity. I walk him three or sometimes four times a day past the aforementioned pale brick nursing home in my neighborhood. While Weegee sniffs the sidewalk, I watch the goings-on at this little facility. I see the occasional family member arriving and departing. I watch elderly residents being wheeled out by attendants. I hear the Caribbean accents of the staff—Jamaican, Haitian, Trinidadian. I see details: a pale blue courtesy curtain hanging in a room. A bulletin board covered in bright orange construction paper announcing the activities for the week in the lobby.

My father suffered from dementia and spent the final years of his life in a nursing home, as did my grandmother. If you've ever hung around a nursing home, it gets you thinking. The experience with my father, my unyielding preoccupation with the nursing home in my neighborhood, combined with a long-held desire to explore the dynamics of an adult brother and sister relationship—somehow led me to *The Savages*.

Once I got down to business, the first draft of *The Savages* took about a year to write and weighed in at a hefty 215 pages. Then I spent another year trying to turn those 215 pages into a manageable screenplay. It was as if I had written a novel and then had to go about the job of adapting it into a screenplay.

After a few days of muffins and coffee and script discussions, the actors and I were no longer meeting in my apartment. Instead, we were showing up at one or another of the many unglamorous locations that made up the story of our movie: parking lots, clapboard houses, hospital rooms, nursing homes, studio apartments, Buffalo streets. And now the actors weren't holding screenplays in their hands as they worked.

During a film shoot, the physical screenplay itself almost disappears from the proceedings. Script pages for the day are shrunken and copied onto small pieces of paper and handed out to everyone on the crew like to-do lists. Once the day is over, these pages are often left behind on the set like discarded little husks. You might find them sitting on top of a monitor or left behind on the dolly. With this image in mind, I find it very poignant to be publishing my screenplay here in book form. Suddenly, it isn't just a practical document for production, it's something with its own—dare I say—literary merit. I am very happy to be presenting it to you here. I hope you enjoy it.

—Tamara Jenkins
November 2007

THE SAVAGES

by

Tamara Jenkins

WHITE SHOOTING SCRIPT – March 17, 2006
BLUE REVISION – April 6, 2006
PINK REVISION – April 10, 2006

1   **EXT. DESERT SUBURBAN DEVELOPMENT - DAY**   1

In dreamy SLOW MOTION, we TRACK down ominously unpeopled streets: ONE-STORY HOUSES in matching pastels float by, ECCENTRIC CACTI shoot up out of GRAVEL LAWNS. TOPIARY GARDENS enhance the unrealness of this place, as do lollipop trees and circular hedges.

Finally, a sign of life as A WOMAN IN A MOTORIZED WHEELCHAIR appears, cheerfully navigating her way along one of the spotless sidewalks.

SUPERTITLE: SUN CITY, ARIZONA

We are floating through America's premiere master-planned retirement community -- a geriatric Eden. As this living brochure continues, we catch glimpses of:

2   -- THE GOLF COURSE   2
where a FEMALE SENIOR tees off as TWO GOLFERS stand by. THWACK!

3   -- THE FIRING RANGE   3
OLD MEN hold rifles and shoot at targets.

4   -- THE POOL   4
A GROUP OF ELDERLY WOMEN in bathing caps rehearse a SYNCHRONIZED SWIMMING ROUTINE a la Esther Williams.

5   -- ON A RESIDENTIAL STREET   5
A handsome ELDERLY COUPLE on A BICYCLE BUILT FOR TWO.

As soon as the bicycle has cleared frame, the CAMERA PICKS OUT A HOUSE and begins to MOVE SLOWLY toward the drawn curtains of the front window. This is one of Sun City's more humble model-home offerings. Eventually we are transported into --

6   **INT. HOUSE - DAY**   6

It's dark in here, but bright sunlight peeks in around the closed drapes making dust particles visible.

Still on the move, the CAMERA locates --

LENNY SAVAGE, 80, sitting at one end of a dining room table, hunched over a bowl of cereal. He is shirtless and moves slowly. Lenny has the labored chewing style of a man who wears dentures, but that does not deter him from indulging in his favorite crunchy cereal: Wheat Chex.

It might be "fun in the sun" for others in this retirement community, but here, where Lenny lives, life ain't so grand.

From another room, A MAN'S VOICE wafts in:

                    MALE VOICE (OS)
          Upsy daisy, thatta girl. We're gonna get
          you out in the nice warm sunshine. Get
          you some vitamin D. D for Doris, right?

THE CAMERA, following the sound of the voice, PANS AWAY
from Lenny and LOOKS DOWN A HALLWAY INTO --

7   **A BEDROOM**   7

Through the door we see an obstructed view of DORIS METZGER,
80, a frail woman sitting on the side of her hospital-style
bed, staring into space. She is being attended to by a home-
health-care worker, EDUARDO, 45, in green surgical scrubs
and a hair-net. He WALKS IN AND OUT of VIEW as he prepares
Doris for her day.

                    EDUARDO
          We're gonna get you all fixed up nice and
          take some pictures for your daughter --

He exits the room HUMMING CHEERFULLY then disappears into
the adjoining doorway of an OFF-SCREEN BATHROOM. His
HUMMING STOPS.

                    EDUARDO (OS) (CONT'D)
          Somebody forgot something in the
          bathroom!

Then, the DISTINCT SOUND OF A TOILET SEAT BANGING against
its porcelain base. Eduardo re-emerges from the bathroom
and marches down the hall and into --

8   **THE DINING ROOM - CONTINUOUS**   8

He stops in front of Lenny.

                    EDUARDO (CONT'D)
          Lenny, you forgot to flush.

There's a tremor in Lenny's voice, but it's aggressive
just the same.

                    LENNY
          I'm eating my cereal, don't ya see?

                    EDUARDO
          I need to use the restroom.

                    LENNY
          So flush it.

Lenny turns his attention back to his bowl.

                    EDUARDO
          I'm not a housekeeper, remember? I'm a
          home-health care professional.

                    LENNY
          Not mine. You're hers. Go bother her.
          I'm eating.

                    EDUARDO
          Take care of your business in the
          bathroom, Mr. Savage.

                    LENNY
          You do it.

                    EDUARDO
          As you already pointed out, you are not
          under my jurisdiction. I am not paid to
          take care of your shit!

Eduardo marches over to Lenny, SNATCHES THE BOWL OF
CEREAL and takes it into the ADJOINING KITCHEN.

                    LENNY
          What the hell are you doing?

Eduardo puts the BOWL inside the REFRIGERATOR.

                    EDUARDO
          Take care of your business in the
          bathroom and then I'll return you your
          Wheat Chex.

Eduardo FLINGS the REFRIGERATOR DOOR SHUT and exits.

THE CAMERA PUSHES IN ON THE REFRIGERATOR where we see --

A MAGNET HOLDING A PHOTO OF DORIS AND LENNY --
on a cruise, in happier and healthier times. They hold
glasses of champagne, frozen in a festive toast.

AT THE DINING TABLE --
Lenny is humiliated and bereft, with only his spoon to
comfort him. He gets up and shuffles out of the room,
revealing that he's not wearing pants, just high-waisted
JOCKEY BRIEFS and a pair of BLACK NYLON KNEE SOCKS.

10   **IN THE BEDROOM --**   10

Through A BUREAU MIRROR, Eduardo opens a jewelry box and slides
rings on Doris's fingers.

                    EDUARDO (CONT'D)
          Are you cleaning up after yourself, Mr.
          Savage?

11   **IN THE BATHROOM --**   11

     Lenny stands in front of the toilet. He stares into the
     open bowl and contemplates its contents.

                    EDUARDO (OS)
          Don't play deaf with me now.

     Lenny glances toward the door with disgust and then looks
     back in the bowl.

     CLOSE ON LENNY'S FACE --
     frozen in an expression of doom. This confrontation with
     his own excrement seems to confirm what Leonard Savage
     already knows to be true -- that his life is shit and
     it's almost over. But then -- What's this? Lenny has an
     idea. A SNEAKY SMILE creeps over his face.

     FROM THE HALLWAY, LOOKING INTO THE BATHROOM --
     Lenny shuffles toward camera and SLAMS the bathroom door
     in our face.

12   **IN THE BEDROOM --**   12

     Eduardo reacts to the sound of the slam.

                    EDUARDO (CONT'D)
          Lenny?

13   **IN THE HALLWAY --**   13

     Eduardo approaches the bathroom door.

                    EDUARDO (CONT'D)
          I didn't hear any flush, Lenny.
                    (knocking)
          Leonard?

     Eduardo waits for a response, then cracks open the door.

                    EDUARDO (CONT'D)
          Leonard?

     EDUARDO'S POV --
     as he swings the door wide open, revealing --

14   **IN THE HALLWAY/BATHROOM --**   14

LENNY --
his hands SMEARED IN BROWN. On the tile wall, in an angry
fecal scrawl, he has written the word: *Prick*. Frightened by
his own actions, Lenny stands there captured and trembling --
staring in disbelief at what he has done and BREATHING HARD.

RING! RING! RING!

15   **INT. NEW YORK APARTMENT - NIGHT**   15

CLOSE ON A RINGING TELEPHONE. The ANSWERING MACHINE
CLICKS ON. The OUTGOING MESSAGE is the voice of --

                    BETTE DAVIS (ON MACHINE)
          Fasten your seatbelts, it's going to be a
          bumpy night.

Then the voice of WENDY SAVAGE comes on.

                    WENDY (ON MACHINE)
          Hello. That was Bette Davis as Margo
          Channing and this is Wendy Savage as
          herself. Leave me a message after the --

BEEP! As the incoming message is recorded, the CAMERA
PANS to reveal a tenement apartment. We see FLEA MARKET
FURNISHINGS, a HISSING RADIATOR and a LARGE, LONELY CAT.

SUPERTITLE: NEW YORK CITY

The camera comes to rest on A PARTIALLY OPEN WINDOW with
blowing sheer curtains that looks out over the streets of
New York City's East Valley on a wintery night.

                    WOMAN'S VOICE
          Aloha, Wendy? This is Nancy Lachman.
          Doris Metzger's daughter. Calling from
          Honolulu... It's been quite a while since
          we've spoken. I'm calling because...
          well... I just got a very disturbing call
          from Arizona. There's been some trouble
          with your Dad --

16   **INT. OFFICE BUILDING - BULLPEN AREA - NIGHT**   16

A large sparsely populated room with many desks and
cubicles. It's after hours. A CLEANING PERSON vacuums.

WENDY SAVAGE, 39, sits at a desk with a scribbled upon
FOLDER before her. On the tab it reads: *FELLOWSHIP AND*
GRANT APPLICATIONS. After a furtive glance around the
room, Wendy types.

                    WENDY (VO)
Dear Selection Committee. If awarded your
prestigious fellowship for artistic
creation, I would use the money to
complete the writing and research of my
new, semi-autobiographical play... No,
wait...
         (backing up the cursor)
...my new...
         (re-typing)
...*subversive*, semi-autobiographical play
about my childhood entitled... WAKE ME
WHEN IT'S OVER.

Wendy glances over the top of her cubicle and SEES the
disembodied HEAD OF MATT, her manager, fast approaching.
With a quick click of her mouse, she brings a SPREADSHEET
up on the computer then covers her FOLDER with AN
ACCOUNTING FILE.

                    MATT
Hey, Wen.

                    WENDY
         (hard working employee act)
Hey, Matt.

                    MATT
How's it going? You getting anywhere?

                    WENDY
Just trying to power through.

                    MATT
Do what you can. Don't kill yourself.

As soon as Matt is gone, A NEIGHBORING FEMALE CO-WORKER
with a pierced lower-lip smirks conspiratorially at
Wendy. Wendy acknowledges the look, but as she returns
to writing her letter it's clear that she wants to
believe she has a higher calling than the other temps.

                    WENDY (VO)
Inspired by the work of Jean Genet, the
cartoons of Lynda Barry and the family
dramas of Eugene O'Neill, WAKE ME WHEN
IT'S OVER, tells the story of a brother
and sister who -- after being abandoned
by their abusive father -- are forced to
fend for themselves when their depressive
mother goes out on a date... from which
she *never returns*...

Accompanying the voice-over is A QUICK MONTAGE:

17   -- AT THE XEROX MACHINE - Wendy makes copies of her   17
applications.

-- AT THE SUPPLY CABINET - She helps herself to PLASTIC
BINDERS, MANILA ENVELOPES and some NICE PENS.

-- AT THE POSTAGE MACHINE - She runs her mailings through
and the names of the recipients flash by: The Guggenheim
Foundation, New Dramatists, The Playwrights Foundation...

18   **EXT. OFFICE BUILDING - NIGHT**   18

Wendy exits, bundled up in a vintage coat and scarf. She
crosses the deserted street and arrives at --

A MAILBOX --
where she removes SEVERAL MANILA ENVELOPES from her satchel.
In a private little ritual, she presses them against her
chest and makes a wish before she drops them inside.

19   **EXT. EAST VALLEY STREET - NIGHT**   19

Wendy walks down the street with a BAG OF TAKE-OUT and
arrives at her APARTMENT BUILDING.

She is about to unlock the front door when it swings open
and a YOUNG EAST VALLEY COUPLE emerge, followed by a
group of their care-free friends. Wendy finds herself
stuck holding the door open as they pass, painfully aware
that they are all at least ten years younger.

As the last friend exits, he thanks Wendy as though she
were a doorman.

20   **INT. WENDY'S APARTMENT - NIGHT**   20

Wendy enters carrying her TAKE-OUT BAG, KEYS and a SMALL
PILE OF MAIL in her teeth.

GENGHIS KHAN, Wendy's cat, jumps off the couch and greets
her with MEOWS. Wendy unloads her stuff, clicks on lights
and pulls off her coat. On her way to feed Genghis, she
wanders over to --

THE TELEPHONE TABLE where the answering machine BLINKS. Wendy
pushes a button. As it plays, she opens a can of cat food.

                  MACHINE'S DIGITAL VOICE
        Mailbox One, there are two new messages.

                              WOMAN'S VOICE
                    Ms. Savage, this is Donna from Dr.
                    Reisman's office. I'm just calling to
                    let you know that your Pap smear results
                    came back today and it's normal,
                    everything is fine. You've got nothing
                    to worry about. If you have any
                    questions, please call the --

A LOUD BUZZER BUZZES.

Wendy, slightly startled, clicks the machine off and, still
holding the can of cat food, heads to the door.

THE CAMERA stays behind, PANNING OFF of Wendy and PUSHING INTO
A CLOSE UP OF THE ANSWERING MACHINE still blinking ominously.

AT THE DOOR --
Wendy presses her eye to the peephole.

THROUGH THE PEEPHOLE --
LARRY, an attractive middle-aged guy, stands in the hall.

With a quick fluff of her hair, Wendy opens the door.

                              WENDY
                    Hi.

                              LARRY
                    Hi.

A strange pause as they stand in the doorway.

                              LARRY (CONT'D)
                    Is this a bad time? I saw your lights
                    come on.

                              WENDY
                    No. I'm just...you know...

                              LARRY
                    Oh, okay, then I don't want to disturb...

                              WENDY
                    No. Do. I mean, if you can. Can you?

Larry nods yes and smiles -- a naughty gleam in his eye.

                              LARRY
                    I got Marley.

Wendy looks down to see Marley, AN OLD GOLDEN LAB with a
greying muzzle. Wendy smiles at Marley and opens the
door to let them in.

A MOMENT LATER --

THE CAMERA PUSHES IN FAST -- Larry has Wendy up against a
wall and is kissing her hungrily, undoing her pants and
pulling at her clothes.

>   WENDY
>   (coming up for air)
>   Let's go to the bed.

He continues to devour her.

>   LARRY
>   I like it here. Let's do it on the floor.

He slides to the floor and tries to pull her down with him.

>   WENDY
>   No, come on Larry.

>   LARRY
>   I need you. Feel how hard my cock is.

Wendy is disgusted. She pulls away from him.

>   WENDY
>   I don't want to. The floor is gross.

Wendy turns and begins to toss pillows off the nearby
FUTON COUCH.

>   LARRY
>   You used to like it on the floor -- when
>   you first moved in, remember?

>   WENDY
>   Yeah, well, not any more.

In a well practiced maneuver, she yanks at the base of
the couch, pulling it forward -- FLUMP! -- transforming
it into a bed.

>   WENDY (CONT'D)
>   It's middle-aged and depressing. It
>   makes me want to cry.

Without a trace of romance, Wendy begins to remove her
shirt.

>   LARRY
>   What's the matter?

Wendy shakes her head, dismissing the question. Marley wants to climb up onto the bed but is too arthritic to manage so Wendy hoists her up by her haunches. She plops down next to Marley and Larry sits down beside her.

> LARRY (CONT'D)
> What?

> WENDY
> I've got things going on.

> LARRY
> What things?

> WENDY
> Just things, Larry. Things. It's personal.

> LARRY
> (kissing her neck)
> I thought this was personal.

> WENDY
> It's personal medical, okay? It's cervical.

Larry stops kissing her neck and gives Wendy his full attention.

> WENDY (CONT'D)
> I had a Pap Smear. Something was irregular. And then I had to have another Pap Smear. They just called with the results --

> LARRY
> And -- ?

Wendy wants special attention -- even if it means fabricating tragedy.

> WENDY
> And it's... not, you know, for sure yet, but they might have to go in and take something out to test and see if it's... you know, God forbid...

Larry presses his head against her chest and rubs her belly protectively.

> LARRY
> I'm sorry, Wen.

Wendy basks in the affection, UNTIL --

                              LARRY (CONT'D)
          Annie had that.

                              WENDY
          What?

                              LARRY
          A cervical thing. Some kind of
          procedure.

Wendy looks at him, her disbelief mounting.

                              LARRY (CONT'D)
          I went with her to the appointment. She
          said it was pretty painless. A little
          sore afterwards, but basically--

                              WENDY
          I really don't need to hear about your
          wife's cervix, right now.

                              LARRY
          I'm trying to be comforting.

                              WENDY
          Yeah, well it's not. It's upsetting.

                              LARRY
          Okay. Sorry.

                              WENDY
          God.

A silent moment as they just sit there side-by-side.

                              LARRY
          Do you want me to go?

Wendy shakes her head no.

                                              CUT TO:

OVERHEAD CLOSE-UP of Wendy with Larry on top, moving
rhythmically. She tries to get lost in the sex but can't.
She opens her eyes and looks at the ceiling. After a few
moments, she turns her head and finds herself staring into
the sad eyes of Marley. She reaches for a paw. Wendy and
Marley stay like that gazing into each other's eyes while
Larry fucks her.

LATER --

Larry pulls his clothes on in semi-darkness. Wendy and
Marley spoon in bed.

LARRY (CONT'D)
C'mon Marley.

Marley licks Wendy's face, hobbles off the bed and joins
Larry.

LARRY (CONT'D)
Goodnight.

Wendy watches from the bed as Larry and Marley leave.

25   STILL LATER --   25

Wendy shuffles out of the kitchen eating her take-out. She
PASSES the TELEPHONE TABLE and notices --

THE RED BLINKING LIGHT of the answering machine. Then,
AN E.C.U. of the red blinking light fills the screen.

26   **EXT. HOUSE - NIGHT**   26

A modest clapboard home with a sagging porch and mounds
of dirty snow surrounding it. Somewhere inside a phone
is RINGING.

SUPERTITLE: BUFFALO

27   **INT. BEDROOM - NIGHT**   27

JONATHAN SAVAGE, 42, is in bed, half-asleep, trying to
ignore the ringing phone. Next to him, where a lover
might be, there is a pile of work: LAP-TOP, PAPERS, EYE
GLASSES, BOOKS. With a groan, he finally gives in and
answers.

JON
Hello?

WENDY (ON PHONE)
Jon, it's me.

Jon looks at THE CLOCK on his nightstand. It's 1:10 am.

JON
What's going on?

WENDY (ON PHONE)
Dad is writing on the walls with his
shit!

                         JON
          What?

INT. WENDY'S APARTMENT - SAME TIME

Wendy paces as she talks, a cigarette clenched between
her fingers. During their conversation, WE INTERCUT.

                         WENDY
          He's writing with his shit, Jon. Words
          on the bathroom wall and he's leaving
          them there for this guy Eduardo to find
          like messages.

Jon snaps on a light.

                         JON
          Wendy, what the fuck are you talking
          about?

                         WENDY
          I am talking about Dad!

                         JON
          Okay.

                         WENDY
          There's something wrong with him. I got
          a phone call. He's losing his mind or
          something. He's acting out with his
          shit. It's all he's got left and he's
          using it to piss this guy off.

                         JON
          What guy?

                         WENDY
          Doris's caregiver guy. Here, listen.

                         JON
          No.

Wendy fumbles with the ANSWERING MACHINE. She CLICKS IT
ON and holds the PHONE to the SPEAKER.

                         ANSWERING MACHINE
          Aloha, Wendy? This is Nancy --

Wendy pushes the FAST FORWARD BUTTON. We HEAR the HIGH
PITCHED CHIPMUNK SOUND.

Jon holds his head in his hand like it's going to
explode.

Wendy releases the button --

                    ANSWERING MACHINE (CONT'D)
          I know you haven't communicated with your
          father for quite some time. He's not the
          same anymore. He forgets things and...
          I'm sorry to leave this on a machine, but
          Eduardo found Lenny this morning...
          handling his...
                    (grasping for propriety)
          ...fecal matter.

                    JON
          Wendy!

                    ANSWERING MACHINE
          We hired Eduardo to care for our mother,
          not your father --

                    JON
          Wendy!!

                    WENDY
                    (phone back to ear)
          What?

                    JON
          Turn it off!

Wendy CLICKS IT OFF.

                    WENDY
          What is your problem?

                    JON
          It's the middle of the night. I've got
          to teach in the morning and I'm on a
          deadline.

                    WENDY
          He's writing with his shit, Jon! Our
          father! Don't leave me alone with this.

                    JON
          I'm not leaving you alone, I'm just
          hanging up. We'll talk tomorrow.

                    WENDY
          We don't even know where the man lives
          anymore. You want to know where he
          lives? Sun City. Have you ever heard of
          that? In the middle of the desert
          somewhere. We're gonna have to go out
          there and find him.

                         JON
          Wendy, we are <u>not</u> going to have to go out
          there and find him. We are not in a Sam
          Shepard play!

                         WENDY
          We have to do <u>something</u>. This is a
          crisis.

                         JON
          Look, I'm not sure if this actually
          qualifies as a crisis. It's an alarm,
          okay. But it's not a crisis. Not yet.

                         WENDY
                    (after a reflective pause)
          You mean it's like we're in orange?

                         JON
          What--? Yeah, right. Exactly. But
          we're only in yellow, okay. So we should
          just... be aware and be...cautious. When
          it hits red, then we're in trouble.

29   **INT. SYLVIA'S NAIL SALON - DAY**   29

       CLOSE ON A BOTTLE OF RED NAIL POLISH as it is held up by
       a KOREAN MANICURIST. She speaks in broken English.

                         MANICURIST
          Your color? Right, Miss Metzger?

       Across from the manicurist, Doris stares at the bottle,
       but says nothing.

                         MANICURIST (CONT'D)
          Ravishing Red, right?

       The manicurist sighs, and begins shaking the bottle of
       nail polish. She turns and speaks to her CO-WORKER in
       Korean.

       The manicurist takes one of Doris's hands, quickly paints
       a nail and holds it up in front of Doris's face.

                         MANICURIST (CONT'D)
          See. You like? Sexy, right?

       Doris stares at her painted nail. Finally, she manages to
       squeeze out the smallest of nods. The manicurist is pleased.

                         MANICURIST (CONT'D)
          Ah, good. See. Good color.

WIDE --
A PLATOON OF KOREAN MANICURISTS in matching aprons attend to
the nails of female customers. A LOUD T.V. plays JUDGE JUDY.

AT THE PEDICURE AREA --
Eduardo sleeps in a LARGE VIBRATING MASSAGE CHAIR. His
feet soak in a low sink of swirling water.

BACK TO THE MANICURE AREA --
The manicurist is still speaking to her friend as she works.
The CAMERA watches the action from a position level with the
table and Doris's hands when suddenly -- like a medicine ball
from outer space --

DORIS'S HEAD drops INTO FRAME --
landing on the table with a THUMP! She arrives FACING
THE CAMERA, EYES OPEN, MOTIONLESS and DEAD.

The SOUND OF A JET grows louder and louder, transporting
us to --

30   **INT. PHOENIX SKY HARBOR AIRPORT - DAY**   30

Jon, pulling his CARRY-ON, paces back and forth at an ARRIVAL
GATE, talking into his CELLPHONE. A flight has just arrived
and PASSENGERS are streaming out the jetway door.

                    JON
          Andy. It's me, Jon. Good. Good. I'm
          still plugging away on that Brecht book.
          Yeah, well, he's a complex man. And
          you?

Wendy emerges from the jetway, spots her brother and hurries
over.

                    WENDY
          Hi Jon.

Wendy tries to kiss him hello, but Jon holds up an index
finger.

                    JON
               (into phone)
          Yeah, I heard Stanford is playing footsie
          with you. Great. Great.

Jon beckons Wendy to follow him as he walks away from the
gate into the terminal. Wendy obeys, annoyed.

                    JON (CONT'D)
               (into phone)
          Look, I need a favor.
               (MORE)

JON (CONT'D)
It's kind of last minute. I'm out of
town, actually... Arizona. Yeah. It's a
family thing. No, nothing serious.

Wendy raises her eyebrows at Jon. He ignores her.

JON (CONT'D)
(into phone)
It's my father... No, he's just... His
girlfriend died. Yeah. And he's getting
pretty old himself, I guess, like everybody.
Yeah, well, that's what I was going to ask
you. It's my nine A.M. on Monday --
Oedipal Rage in Beckett of all things.

WENDY
(tugging on Jon's arm)
I've got to go to baggage claim.

JON
(into phone)
Hold on a sec.
(to Wendy, covering phone)
You checked luggage? We're only here for
a day.

WENDY
Two days and one night. Excuse me if I
plan on changing my clothes.

Wendy scans Jon's sloppy outfit with her eyes. Jon
returns his attention to the phone.

JON
Sorry about that... My sister...

31   **EXT. RENTAL CAR PARKING LOT - DAY**   31

Jon loads the trunk of a rented MALIBU while Wendy
examines his outfit.

WENDY
Is that what you're going to wear?

Jon looks at his clothes -- a long-john T-shirt and cargo
pants -- then back at Wendy, confused.

WENDY (CONT'D)
To pay *respect*?

Irritated, he yanks off his shirt, unzips his bag and
digs around for something more appropriate.

                              JON
                    I gained some weight.

                              WENDY
                    I didn't say anything.
                         (looking in his suitcase)
                    Kasia didn't have you pack a button-down?

                              JON
                    What is this, a goddamn fashion show?

                              WENDY
                    No, it's just that when someone dies
                    people dress up.

Jon pulls a shirt from deep inside his bag and puts it on.

                              JON
                    She's moving back to Poland.

                              WENDY
                    You and Kasia broke up?

                              JON
                         (buttoning up his shirt)
                    Her visa expired.

He presents himself to Wendy. She nods in vague approval.
Jon SLAMS the trunk CLOSED.

                              WENDY
                    So that's it. Her visa expires and
                    it's over?

They walk to the front of the car, Jon to the driver's side.

                              JON
                    We'll it's either that or we get married
                    and nobody is ready for that.

They climb into the car.

32   **INT. RENTAL CAR - DAY**   32

As they buckle in --

                              WENDY
                    You've been going out for three years.
                    You're forty-two years old. Don't you
                    think --

                    JON
        Wendy! I really don't need romantic advice
        from my little sister at the moment. Let's
        just take care of this situation and stay
        out of each other's shit. Okay?

                    WENDY
        I'm just trying to talk about it.

                    JON
        Well, we're not in therapy right now.
        We're in real life.

                    WENDY
        Okay. Geez.

Jon starts the engine and pulls away.

33   **EXT. DESERT HIGHWAY - DAY**   33

      The rental car whizzes by.

34   **INT./EXT. CAR - DESERT HIGHWAY - DAY (MOVING)**   34

      Jon drives, Wendy shotgun. Ahead is the OPEN ROAD.
      Above, THE HUGE DESERT SKY. AN EXIT SIGN reads: Sun
      City. Jon takes the exit.

35   **INT./EXT. CAR - ROAD - DAY (MOVING)**   35

      Wendy and Jon watch the surreal sights of Sun City sail past.

36   **INT./EXT. DORIS METZGER'S STREET - RENTAL CAR**   36

      They round a corner and park in front of DORIS
      METZGER'S HOUSE. The siblings stare at the house with
      trepidation.

                    JON
        This is going to be weird.

                    WENDY
        Yeah. I wonder what he looks like.
                (remembering something)
        Oh shoot! I almost forgot.

Wendy digs through her purse and pulls out a HALLMARK
SYMPATHY CARD.

                    WENDY (CONT'D)
We have to sign this. They didn't have a
very big selection. Do you think this is
okay?
          (reading the message)
These words we hope may ease your loss.
Our prayers are with you. Our love. Our
thoughts.

Jon stares at his sister in disbelief.

                    WENDY (CONT'D)
So this is sent in sympathy...

Jon impatiently grabs the card, leans it against the
steering wheel and signs it.

37   **EXT. DORIS'S HOUSE - DAY**   37

The siblings walk up the path toward the house with sad
gift shop offerings: Jon with the string of A FOIL
BALLOON that reads, "We Love Dad," Wendy with CELLOPHANE
WRAPPED FLOWERS. They arrive at --

THE SCREEN DOOR
Jon pushes the DOORBELL. No response.
Wendy presses her face up to the screen and looks inside.

WENDY'S POV of THE FOYER --
Her eyes land on an ALUMINUM WALKER.

Jon KNOCKS lightly on the screen.

                    JON
Hello. Dad?

                    EDUARDO (O.S.)
Coming!

Eduardo appears on the other side of the screen door. It's
obvious from his surprised expression and the fact that he
doesn't open the door right away that something is amiss.

                    EDUARDO (CONT'D)
You must be Leonard's kids.

                    WENDY
Uh-huh.

                    EDUARDO
Didn't you get my message?

38   **INT. METZGER LIVING ROOM - DAY**   38

Jon and Wendy sit side-by-side on the couch with uncertain
expressions on their faces. The pathetic balloon floats
above them. FLOWERS and SYMPATHY CARDS abound.

Across from them -- NANCY LACHMAN, 47, sits with her
husband, BILL, 48, who nurses a Heineken. Their
children, HOPE and FAITH are nearby watching "SpongeBob
SquarePants" on the T.V. Eduardo hovers.

                    NANCY
          The hospital is just five minutes away. And
          don't worry. It's nothing serious. He'd
          been feeling kind of faint and what with the
          toileting incident and all, the doctor
          thought a few tests were in order.

                    EDUARDO
          I told him I didn't think there was
          anything wrong with that man's mind.
          That it was just Lenny being Lenny. But
          he insisted on taking a look for himself.

                    JON
               (to Nancy)
          So when did he go there?

                    NANCY
          Um --

                    EDUARDO
          Just last night. I'm sorry you didn't get
          my message.

                    JON
          Well, I guess we should be going then.

Jon and Wendy rise, awkwardly gathering their things.
Wendy remembers their card and hands it to Nancy.

                    WENDY
          We're really sorry about your mom.

                    NANCY
          Thank you.

Bill gives Nancy a look, encouraging her to speak up.

                    NANCY (CONT'D)
          Uh, Jon, Wendy... One more thing. Before
          you go. Please, sit. I just want to
          say...
               (MORE)

                              NANCY (CONT'D)
                          (getting choked up)
                    You know, we love Lenny. He's been like
                    family to us...

Wendy and Jon sit again, smiling gratefully.

                              NANCY (CONT'D)
                    But he's not *really* our family. He's yours.

Jon and Wendy's smiles evaporate.

                              NANCY (CONT'D)
                    So, I hope you'll be able to find some
                    place nice for him.

                              JON
                    What do you mean?

                              BILL
                    She means a place where he can live.

                              JON
                    He lives here.

                              BILL
                    That's correct. Your father <u>has</u> <u>been</u>
                    living off the charity of our family for
                    quite some time.

                              NANCY
                    Bill --

Uh-oh. Jon instantly understands what's happening, but
Wendy is baffled.

                              JON
                    Why would you say charity, Bill? Doris
                    asked my father to come live with her as
                    a boyfriend not a boarder. They were a
                    couple. They were together for over
                    twenty years.

Nancy starts to cry. Twelve-year-old Hope drifts over and
protectively attaches herself to her mother's leg. She stares
suspiciously at Wendy and Jon. Wendy smiles nervously at the
glaring child.

                              JON (CONT'D)
                    You can't just throw the man out on the
                    street. He has a right to live here.
                    Legally speaking. It's a common law
                    marriage at this point.

                              BILL
                    Well, not exactly...

                         NANCY
                (glancing at her husband)
            Not in front of the kids, Bill.

Bill rises, hitches up his pants and picks up his VALISE.

                         BILL
                     (to Jon)
            Why don't we step outside.

Jon gets up warily and hands off the balloon to Wendy. Bill
leads Jon across the room, rolls open a GLASS DOOR and the
two men step out into a PATIO AREA. Bill slides the door
closed behind them.

Wendy and Nancy sit silently watching them. After a
moment, Nancy turns and smiles at Wendy. Wendy smiles
back. It is excruciatingly awkward.

39   THROUGH THE CLOSED SLIDING GLASS DOORS -   39
      Bill and Jon talk animatedly. Bill pulls a DOCUMENT from
      his valise and hands it to Jon. Jon puts on a PAIR OF
      GLASSES. Bill takes a swig from a bottle of Heineken and
      watches him read.

                         JON (PRE-LAP)
            It's called a Non-marital Agreement. It's
            something Doris had drafted up years ago.

40   **EXT. DORIS' HOUSE - DAY**   40

      AGITATED HAND-HELD as Wendy and Jon march down the path,
      their balloon in tow. Jon grips a copy of the document.

                         JON
            It's like a pre-nup without the nup. It
            says that even though they live together
            they have no legal obligation to each
            other. That everything is separate. And
            basically that Dad has no right to any of
            her property. I bet they've already got
            the place listed.

                         WENDY
            Did you notice that there wasn't one
            picture of us anywhere? It's like we
            don't even exist.

41   **INT. HOSPITAL THIRD FLOOR - DAY**   41

Wendy and Jon hustle down a long hall, VISITOR STICKERS
affixed to their shirts. They each carry a cup from
Starbucks. Their foil balloon bounces overhead.

Checking the room numbers, they slow down as they
approach the one they seek. Jon makes sure Wendy is
ready before he reaches for the knob.

42   **INT. HOSPITAL ROOM - DAY**   42

A T.V. suspended from the ceiling plays a LOUD GAME SHOW.
Jon and Wendy quietly enter and step around a curtain to
find --

LENNY, asleep, with an IV in his arm.

They stand there a moment, haggardly staring at their
estranged and ailing father.   Then --

                    JON
          Wen?

                    WENDY
          What?

Jon nods at something on the other side of the bed.
Wendy looks and SEES A BAG WITH DARK YELLOW LIQUID
hanging from a stand.

                    JON
          Dad's taking a piss.

Wendy and Jon stare blankly as the liquid level RISES. A
strange pause. Then A BURST OF APPLAUSE from the T.V.

Wendy and Jon look up at the T.V. It's JEOPARDY. They
watch for a long spaced out moment. In unison, they take
a sip from their Starbucks. Then--

                    LENNY (O.S)
          Where the hell have you been?

Wendy and Jon turn to face Lenny.

                    WENDY & JON
          Hi Dad. Hi. How are you doing?

                    LENNY
          They've had me hog-tied for two days.
          Can't you see?

Lenny becomes agitated and starts to thrash around. His
sheet slides off to reveal RESTRAINTS holding his wrists
and ankles. Wendy and Jon look at each other, horrified.

> WENDY
> We just got here. We came pretty much
> straight from the airport. It's Wendy
> and Jon.

Lenny eyes his children.

> LENNY
> I know who you are. You're the late
> ones. You're late! You weren't here!
> And this is what they do, see.

Lenny pulls violently against his restraints.

> JON
> Dad! Dad! Stop.

Lenny doesn't stop. He's wild.

> WENDY
> (shrinking away from the bed)
> Jon, go get somebody.

> LENNY
> You weren't here, I said! Nobody!

> JON
> (grabbing his father's arm)
> Dad!

Lenny stops momentarily and stares up at his son. A tiny
flicker of fear in his eyes.

> JON (CONT'D)
> We weren't here because we live on the
> east coast. Remember? We haven't seen
> you in a long time. We came here to help
> you.

> LENNY
> So do something. You're the doctor.

> WENDY
> He's not that kind of doctor, Dad. He's
> a professor.

> JON
> (to Wendy)
> I'm gonna go get somebody.

Jon goes to the door and exits.

> LENNY
> I thought my boy was a doctor.

> WENDY
> Doctor of Philosophy. PhD. Jon teaches
> college.

> LENNY
>
> Medicine?

> WENDY
> No. Drama. He teaches theater.

> LENNY
> Like Broad-way? Zasu Pitts?

> WENDY
> No, like... "Theater of Social Unrest."
> Stuff like that. He's doing a book on
> Bertolt Brecht.

The door swings open. In walks Jon with a NURSE.

> NURSE
> I'll untie him only if he promises to be
> good. He can't be trying to get out of bed
> by himself. You gonna be good, Mr. Savage?

> JON
> Dad, are you gonna be good? If you're
> not good they won't untie you.

Lenny stays still and stares at his son like an obedient
dog who wants his reward.

> NURSE
> You can't go pulling on everything, now.
> (re: IV tube)
> This here is for your own good. This is
> your food.
> (untying his hands and feet)
> We can't have him climbing out on his
> own. He's unsteady and he can fall.

> JON
> We'll keep an eye on him.

The nurse exits the room. Now untied, Lenny looks up at
Wendy and Jon suspiciously. Everyone just stands there,
unsure what's supposed to happen next.

> DOCTOR (PRE-LAP)
> Vascular dementia or multi-infarct,
> usually follow one or more strokes. But
> I don't see any signs of a stroke here.
> No tumor.

43   **INT. HOSPITAL FILM VIEWING ROOM**   43

DARKNESS. Then, A DOOR OPENS allowing some light into A
ROOM. A DOCTOR, Wendy and Jon enter.

> DOCTOR
> But the disinhibition; the aggression,
> the "masked face" with the blank stare we
> talked about; slowness of speech, memory
> loss. These are all fairly good
> indicators.

CLICK. CLICK. CLICK. Lights stutter on and --

A SERIES OF MRI PICTURES OF LENNY'S BRAIN --
appear one at a time as wall-mounted light boxes are
switched on.   We are in --

> WENDY
> Is it like Alzheimer's?

> DOCTOR
> There are lots of different illnesses
> that cause dementia and I'm not prepared
> to make a diagnosis yet, but to my mind
> your father's symptoms seem more
> characteristic of Parkinson's Disease.

> JON
> So what do we have to look forward to?

> DOCTOR
> If I'm right, then tremors -- when the
> limb is at rest. A shuffling walk.
> Freezing up, unable to initiate
> movement...

As the doctor speaks, Wendy and Jon look around at the
dark mysterious images of their father's brain. The
HUMMING OF THE LIGHT BOXES increases, eventually drowning
out the doctor's voice.

44   **EXT. BEST WESTERN INN OF SUN CITY - DUSK**   44

The BLUE AND YELLOW SIGN glows against the desert sky, accompanied by a DUET, sung by an older man and woman.

> DUET
> *You make me feel so young. You make me feel that spring is sprung...*

The SONG continues over --

45   **EXT. CORRIDOR BEST WESTERN - NIGHT**   45

Wendy and Jon roll their bags toward their room. PALM TREES silhouetted against the sky sway in the desert breeze.

> DUET
> *Every time I see you grin, I'm such a happy individual...*

46   **INT. BEST WESTERN LOUNGE - NIGHT**   46

BURT & LIZZY -- a low-rent Steve and Eydie Gormet are singing the duet we've been hearing. The AUDIENCE OF RETIREES love them.

AT THE BAR --
Wendy and Jon are drinking sodas and eating nuts. Wendy leafs through a pamphlet called "Dementia" while Jon peruses "Parkinson's Disease."

> WENDY
> Maybe Dad didn't abandon us. Maybe he just forgot who we were.

> JON
> I'm going to give Brian Deener a call.

> WENDY
> Who's that?

> JON
> A friend of mine. Teaches in the English Department. He just put his mother in a nursing home near campus...
> (to bartender)
> Can we get some more nuts?

Wendy looks at Jon, stunned.

                         WENDY
          A nursing home?

                         JON
          Yeah. What?

                         WENDY
          I don't know. I wasn't thinking about
          putting him in a nursing home.

                         JON
          Well, what were you thinking?

                         WENDY
          I don't know, but I wasn't thinking that.

                         JON
          Well, what then?

                         WENDY
          I don't know, Jon! I just said. It's
          just not what I was picturing is all.

                         JON
          Where else is he going to live, Wen? I
          mean really -- what's the alternative?
          You want to change Dad's diapers and wipe
          his ass? I don't.

An OLDER COUPLE at a neighboring table look over. Wendy
smiles at them and lowers her voice.

                         WENDY
          He doesn't need diapers, Jon.

                         JON
          Well what do you think that catheter was?

                         WENDY
          That's just because he's in the hospital.

                         JON
          Look, even if they did let Dad stay here,
          he'd still need somebody to take care of
          him. And you know we can't afford that.
          And you heard the nurse, Dad falls. He's
          disoriented --

                         WENDY
          Dad hasn't fallen since we've been here.

                         JON
          That's 'cause he's lying down in a
          hospital!
                         (MORE)

                         JON (CONT'D)
          Don't make me out to be the evil brother
          who is putting our father away against
          your will. We're doing this together,
          right?

Wendy pokes her ice with a cocktail straw.

                         WENDY
          What about those places?

                         JON
          What places?

                         WENDY
          Like Aunt Gertie.

                         JON
          That's assisted living. I'm not sure
          Dad'll get into one of them. Gertie was
          pretty independent, remember? She was
          also rich.
                    (pause)
          Look, there's no one else here to help us
          with this. It's just us. We have to do
          this thing together, right?
                    (no response)
          Wendy?

                         WENDY
          No, yeah, you're right, of course.

                         JON
          Okay. So, I'm going to call United and try
          to get the first flight out of here
          tomorrow morning so I can get back and
          start looking for a place that'll take him.

                         WENDY
          What am I going to do?

                         JON
          You're going to have to stay here and
          hold down the fort until I find
          something.

                         WENDY
          By myself?

                         JON
          Wendy, this is not the time to regress.

                         PRE-LAP
          "Whhhaaaaa!!!"

47   **INT. BEST WESTERN - ROOM - NIGHT**   47

LUCILLE BALL bawls like a baby in an episode of
I LOVE LUCY. Across from the TV, Wendy is in bed,
sleeping. Mixed in with the sound of the television, we
hear Jon talking -- upset mumbling coming from the
bathroom. Wendy's eyes flutter open.

WENDY'S POV --
A sliver of Jon through the bathroom door. He's on the
phone. We can't make out all the words, but it's clear
that he's having some kind of disagreement with his
girlfriend. After a moment, he hangs up. HOLD ON him
standing silent and still over the sink. Then, a spasm of
short little breaths and he starts to cry.

Wendy is moved by this vision of her brother's vulnerability.
She closes her eyes again, as we --

                                            FADE TO BLACK.

48   UNDER BLACK --   48

                         JON
                      (hushed)
                Hey, Wendy. Wen. Wen.

FADE IN TO SEE WENDY'S POV --
of Jon, standing over the bed, all dressed with his
luggage hanging off him. It's still dark outside.

ANGLE ON BLEARY-EYED WENDY --
twisted up in bedclothes looking up at Jon.

                         WENDY
                What?

                         JON
                I'm going.

Wendy sleepily watches as Jon pulls out some cash and
places it on the bureau.

                      JON (CONT'D)
                That should take care of the hotel.

                         WENDY
                Thanks.

Jon nods and heads for the door.

                      WENDY (CONT'D)
                Jon?

                    JON
          Yeah?

                    WENDY
          Are you okay?

                    JON
          Yeah, I'm fine. I'll call you.

Jon leaves, pulling the door closed behind him, leaving
Wendy in the dark, her anxious face barely visible.

49   **INT. BEST WESTERN ROOM - MORNING**   49

      MUSIC PUMPS. ON THE T.V. an exercise program plays.
      Wendy is in her underwear, struggling to follow along.
      She feels pathetic, but pushes herself to do it anyway.

50   **INT. LARRY'S APARTMENT - DAY**   50

      CLOSE ON A RINGING PHONE. In the background, Larry looks
      up from his spot at the kitchen table. Before he can get
      up, his wife ANNIE answers.

                    ANNIE
          Hello?

51   **INT. BEST WESTERN ROOM - DAY**   51

      Wendy, sweaty from her work-out, holds the phone, but
      doesn't speak.

                    ANNIE (ON PHONE)
          Hello? Who is it? Hello? Hello?

      The CLICKING SOUND OF HANGING UP. Wendy stares into
      space, hating her life.

52   **EXT. DORIS' HOUSE - DAY**   52

      A SMALL BANNER that says "OPEN HOUSE" hangs out front
      flapping in the dry breeze.

53   **INT. DORIS' HOUSE - DAY**   53

      SEVERAL ELDERLY COUPLES ARE being shown around by a REAL
      ESTATE AGENT who does her pitch. The CAMERA LOCATES an
      open doorway and peeks into --

54   **THE GUEST ROOM --**   54

where Wendy can be seen unzipping a large, cheap
SUITCASE. She props it open on a couch.

We MOVE INSIDE the room as Wendy pushes open the
accordion doors of a large closet to reveal a sad
assortment of MEN'S CLOTHES. After a moment reflecting
upon the sorry state of her father's life, Wendy removes
an armful of clothes, hangers and all, and dumps them
into the suitcase.

55   **IN THE BATHROOM --**   55

A DRAWER OPENS, LINED WITH FLORAL CONTACT PAPER --
Miscellaneous toiletries slide around inside. Wendy's
hand rifles through the items, removing anything "Male".

A MEDICINE CABINET OPENS, PACKED WITH PHARMACEUTICALS --
Wendy's hand quickly extracts all the vials on which Leonard
Savage's name appears. The cabinet CLOSES.

Suddenly Wendy re-opens the cabinet. Her fingers drift
over the pill bottles until they locate one that says:
Doris Metzger -- and below that: *Percocet*. Wendy takes
the bottle and shuts the cabinet again.

IN THE MIRROR, we see her remove a pill, pop it in her
mouth and wash it back with a handful of water.

56   **IN THE LIVING ROOM --**   56

Wendy drags suitcases toward the front door, passing the
REAL ESTATE AGENT who, having released the group of
buyers, rattles around the house by herself, talking on
her cell phone. She sees Wendy, covers her phone and
whispers --

                    REAL ESTATE AGENT
          I'm sorry about your loss.

57   **EXT./INT. CAB - MOVING**   57

Wendy, feeling the narcotic effects of the Percocet, leans
against the window and looks out at the strange desert
landscape blurring by.

58   **INT. BEST WESTERN - DAY**   58

SUITCASES filled with Lenny's belongings are parked
around the room.

Wendy sits on the bed looking through the contents of an
OLD BRIEFCASE -- bundles of LETTERS, yellowed children's
DRAWINGS and an assortment of WALLET-SIZED SCHOOL
PORTRAITS of Wendy and Jon. The PHONE RINGS and Wendy
answers.

                    WENDY
          Hello?

59   **EXT. BUFFALO STREET - DAY**   59

It's bitterly cold. Jon wears a MASSIVE PARKA and paces
with his cell phone pressed to his ear. His breath is
visible and rushes out of his mouth as he speaks.

                    JON
          Hi.

INTERCUT between Wendy and Jon.

                    WENDY
          Oh my god, Jon, you're not going to
          believe it. I just found this stash of
          pictures of us from Dewey Elementary. I
          can't believe he kept them all this time.

She fishes out a goofy photo of Jon.

                    WENDY (CONT'D)
          I am looking at the funniest picture of
          you, right now...

                    JON
               (shivering, but amused)
          Oh yeah?

                    WENDY
          With a big mouth full of metal. How come
          you got braces, they never gave me
          braces?

                    JON
          Have you ever looked at my teeth?
          They're still crooked.

                    WENDY
          Yeah. How come?

                         JON
             'Cause Dad never paid the bills and the
             orthodontist was so pissed, he pulled the
             braces out of my mouth before my teeth
             were fixed.

Wendy snort-laughs.

                         JON (CONT'D)
             So, I think I found something.

                         WENDY
             What?

                         JON
             A place with an opening that can take him
             right away.

                         WENDY
             What kind of place?

                         JON
                  (sarcastic)
             A facility for older people. In this
             country we call them nursing homes.

                         WENDY
             I thought we were gonna try assisted
             living.

                         JON
             They're not going to take him in assisted
             living, Wendy! Let's be real. He's got
             dementia.

                         WENDY
             Well don't lead with that.

                         JON
             Look, if it's any consolation -- this
             place -- they don't call it a nursing
             home.

                         WENDY
             What do they call it?

                         JON
             A Rehabilitation Center. It's called The
             Valley View.

The CAMERA PANS AWAY to reveal that Jon is standing near
the very place he speaks of. It is a grim institutional
building with a sign out front, *The Valley View
Rehabilitation Center.*

                    WENDY
          That sounds nice. Is it?

                    JON
          It's a nursing home, Wendy!

                    WENDY
          Does it smell?

                    JON
          Yes, Wendy it smells. They all smell.
          Look, this place has an empty bed, they
          take Medicaid and it's close to my house.
          Believe me, once you get inside these
          places, they're all the same.

Wendy holds the phone unable to speak for a long moment.

                    JON (CONT'D)
          Wendy?

                    WENDY
          Make sure to have a coat for him when we
          get there. He doesn't have any warm
          clothes.

60   **INT. HOSPITAL - DAWN**   60

Viewed from behind, Wendy hustles down an empty corridor.

61   **INT. LENNY'S HOSPITAL ROOM - DAWN**   61

Wendy enters and sees the empty hospital bed and no sign
of anything else at first. Then she steps deeper into
the room and turns to find --

Lenny, sitting in a wheelchair, all ready to go. He's been
dressed by the nurses and it shows. He wears a FLANNEL SHIRT
with SUSPENDERS, TROUSERS and a BASEBALL CAP, like a kid
dressed for school by somebody else's mother.

Wendy is struck by the poignancy of this but moves on
with the business at hand.

                    WENDY
          Hi Dad.

After a little delay, Lenny pulls his attention away from
the wall he's been staring at and stiffly twists his head
to look at his daughter.

> LENNY
> Hi ya.

There is a glimmer in his eye, a tiny smile on his face. Lenny seems to have some vague feeling of hope, not unlike the way a dog senses that his beloved family is planning a vacation and he might be taken along. Wendy removes Lenny's baseball cap and gives him a kiss on the forehead.

> WENDY
> How're you feeling?

> LENNY
> Not bad.

She tosses the cap on the bed and begins unclipping his suspenders. Lenny does not resist.

> WENDY
> You don't need these, right, Dad? Not
> your style. They're like Grandpa Walton.

62   **INT. HOSPITAL CORRIDOR - DAY**   62

THE NURSES' STATION --
Wendy finishes signing the HOSPITAL RELEASE FORMS, folds the papers in half and shoves them into one of the plastic bags that hang off the back of Lenny's wheelchair.

A NURSE in her 50's hands over Lenny's medical records, medications and instructions. Wendy dumps the pill bottles into her purse.

> NURSE
> Here. Lemme give you some of these.

The nurse looks over her shoulder to make sure she is unobserved, then pulls out a half a dozen ADULT DIAPERS. Wendy's eyes widen.

> NURSE (CONT'D)
> They don't like us to give this stuff
> away, but you might need it.

She hands the diapers to Wendy.

> WENDY
> Thanks.

She stuffs the diapers in her bag.

> WENDY (CONT'D)
> (rousing herself)
> Okay.

Wendy turns the wheelchair, pointing it toward the exit.

> WENDY (CONT'D)
> Ready, Dad?

> LENNY
> Yep.

> NURSE
> Have a good trip, Mr. Savage.
> (whispering to Wendy)
> Good luck.

Lenny waves with a small wiggle of his fingers. Wendy rolls him away.

63   **INT. JETWAY - DAY**   63

We MOVE toward the aircraft. TWO FLIGHT ATTENDANTS stand at the far end by the cabin door.

REVERSE ANGLE --
Wendy pushes Lenny's wheelchair. TWO AIRLINE EMPLOYEES march behind her in matching uniforms. They arrive at the CABIN DOOR, where the flight attendants greet them.

Out of nowhere, the two airline employees produce A FOLDED METAL CONTRAPTION and pull open a series of METAL FLAPS, transforming it into A BOARDING CHAIR. Unlike a wheelchair, it's narrow enough to fit down the aisle of an airplane.

Wendy stands by and watches as they transfer Lenny to the boarding chair. Lenny's beseeching eyes are fixed on Wendy as he is handled by these human furniture movers. They arrange his arms across his chest, straight-jacket style, and strap him in.

Wendy looks on helplessly as Lenny, not unlike a crate on a supermarket dolly, is TILTED BACK, SPUN AROUND and WHEELED onto the aircraft, BACKWARDS.

64   **INT. AIRPLANE - CONTINUOUS**   64

Wendy lumbers down the aisle following behind Lenny, banging passengers with her bags.

> WENDY
> Sorry. Excuse me...

WENDY'S POV of the SEATED PASSENGERS stealing looks at
her and her father as they make their humiliating
pilgrimage to COACH.

AT THEIR ASSIGNED SEATS --

Lenny is helped into the aisle seat while Wendy shoves
their bags into the overhead compartment. She squeezes
past her father and collapses into the WINDOW SEAT.

                                              CUT TO:

65   AN ENDLESS LANDSCAPE OF CLOUDS.   65

ON WENDY --
staring out the window. Suddenly --

THWACK! Lenny slams his hand down on his tray. He's
agitated, scattering what remains of his SNACK BOX. He
begins to tug and fumble with his SEATBELT.

                    WENDY (CONT'D)
               Dad, what are you doing?

Lenny turns stiffly and looks at Wendy.

                    LENNY
                 (flat)
               Bath-room.

                    WENDY
               What?

                    LENNY
                 (agitated and loud)
               BATH-ROOM!

                    WENDY
               Okay, Dad. Calm down. Let's just wait
               for the lady to come and take our stuff
               away so we can --

                    LENNY
               NOW!

Lenny pulls violently on his seatbelt. Wendy glances
over her shoulder and sees the CONCERNED FACES of
neighboring passengers.

                    WENDY
                 (mortified)
               Okay. Okay, Dad we'll take care of it.

She frantically clears off his tray table and latches it to the seatback. Lenny tries to lift himself up.

                    WENDY (CONT'D)
          Not yet, Dad. Just wait a second.

Wendy climbs over her father and stumbles into the aisle. She tucks her hair behind each ear and readies herself.

                    WENDY (CONT'D)
          Okay, Dad --

Wendy takes Lenny's hands and helps him shimmy into the aisle. They stand there, facing each other and holding hands like mismatched dance partners. Wendy starts inching backwards, slowly leading Lenny toward the bathroom.

                    WENDY (CONT'D)
          That's good, Dad.

Suddenly, Lenny stops. His face distressed.

                    WENDY (CONT'D)
          Dad, what?

Wendy looks down and lets out a TINY GASP.

A WIDE SHOT reveals that Lenny's pants have collapsed around his ankles -- he's standing in the middle of the airplane in his diapers. As word spreads, passengers throughout the cabin crane their necks to get a look.

                    WENDY (CONT'D)
          It's okay, Dad. Don't worry. We're
          fine.

Seems like Lenny needed those suspenders after all.

66   **EXT. BUFFALO NIAGARA INT'L AIRPORT - CURBSIDE - NIGHT**   66

Jon's ten year-old TOYOTA CORROLA idles in front of the arrival area. The windows are frosted and steamed up.

Jon sits behind the wheel listening to ALL THINGS CONSIDERED on NPR. Very civilized. Then --

THWAK! SPLAT!

ON THE DRIVER'S SIDE WINDOW --
A HAND APPEARS, wiping away the snow and frost to reveal a frantic Wendy.

                        WENDY
          Jon!

                        JON
               (rolling down the window)
          Hey, Wen.

Wendy hands some PATENT LEATHER LOAFERS through the
window.

                        JON (CONT'D)
          What's this?

                        WENDY
          They're Dad's. I can't get them back on
          his feet. They swelled up.
               (moving toward the trunk)
          Pop the trunk.

Wendy tosses the bags in, slams it shut and returns to
Jon's window.

                        JON
          Where is he?

                        WENDY
          Inside.
               (holding out her hand)
          The coat.

Jon pulls a MASSIVE PARKA from the back seat and shoves
it through the window.

                        JON
          I can't leave the car unattended.

                        WENDY
          Fine.

                        JON
          Is everything alright?

Wendy looks at Jon with a flat expression, then pivots
around and leaves with the parka. Jon looks out the
window.

THROUGH THE MASSIVE PLATE GLASS WINDOW OF THE TERMINAL --
He sees Lenny sitting in an airport wheelchair, parked by
the luggage. Lenny seems to be the only person in the
whole terminal that isn't moving.

ON JON -- watching, the image sinking in -- his father is
a helpless old man.

68   **INT. TOYOTA COROLLA - NIGHT (MOVING)**   68

They're all packed in, Wendy in the back with their carry-
ons. Lenny's face is barely visible inside the fur-lined
hood of the parka. The windshield wipers squeak and push wet
snow from the glass. After a few moments of uncomfortable
silence, Jon steals a glance at his father.

                    JON
      Been a while since you've seen this, huh
      Dad? Snow. What d'you think?

Lenny stares ahead. After a moment --

                    LENNY
      Lousy.

                    JON
      Yeah, it's always like this this time of
      year.

                    LENNY
      Not the weather. Your driving. It's
      lousy. Never could drive.

Wendy starts cracking up in the backseat. Then Jon joins in.

                    LENNY (CONT'D)
         (amused)
      What're you a bunch a dummies? The hell
      you laughing at?

This only makes Jon and Wendy laugh louder. Now Lenny
starts laughing. Everybody is laughing like crazy.
Eventually, the laughter dies down and trails off. A
brief silence, then --

                    LENNY (CONT'D)
      Did anyone of you remember to tell Doris
      I'm outta town for a while? She gets
      worried.

Wendy and Jon nervously glance at each other in the rear
view mirror.

                    JON
      Uh, yeah, Dad, I took care of that.
      Nothing to worry about.

69   **EXT. BUFFALO STREETS - NIGHT (MOVING)**   69

A commercial strip: Low buildings, out-dated stores, fast
food restaurants.

70   **INT./EXT. CAR - NIGHT**   70

As they pull up in front of the VALLEY VIEW, the
ILLUMINATED SIGN flickers. Wendy takes in the building and
its surroundings.

                         WENDY
                   (under her breath)
               Where's the view?

71   **INT. VALLEY VIEW NURSING HOME - NIGHT**   71

Wendy, Jon and Lenny (once again in a borrowed
wheelchair) are being lead through the facility by a
heavy-hipped African-American nurse, MS. ROBINSON. She's
tired but not unkind. Wendy and Jon carry suitcases and
plastic bags with Lenny's things. Lenny cradles a bag in
his lap.

                    MS. ROBINSON
          We don't usually admit new residents after
          five o'clock, but I understand you came a
          long way. Isn't that right Mr. Savage?

                    LENNY
          What'd ya say?

                    MS. ROBINSON
                   (louder)
          You came a long way.

                    LENNY
          Not too bad.

WENDY'S MOVING POV --
The staff is scarce at this down-at-the-heels facility.
Residents are lightly scattered about the communal
spaces. Some are parked in hallways. Others wander.

As they pass A LAUNDRY CART filled with dirty sheets,
Wendy takes a whiff. Her nostrils flare.

Lenny seems unaware of what exactly is happening. His
expression is peaceful, almost dreamy.

A CAT darts across the hall.

                              MS. ROBINSON
                    That's Winston, we call him the Mayor.

72   **ANOTHER HALLWAY --**   72

        Ms. Robinson leads Lenny, Wendy and Jon to --

        ROOM B-26 --
        She knocks lightly. No response. She turns the knob and
        looks back at the Savages --

                              MS. ROBINSON (CONT'D)
                    Here we are.

        She pushes open the door.

73   **INT. ROOM B-26 - CONTINUOUS**   73

        As they pass through the small entranceway --

                              MS. ROBINSON
                         (pointing things out)
                    The bathroom and the closet here you'll
                    share with Mr. Sperry.

        Ms. Robinson ushers everyone past A CURTAINED-OFF BED
        SPACE and into the back half of the room. Lenny, Wendy
        and Jon stop and look around.

        THEIR POV --
        The CAMERA PANS ACROSS a hospital-style bed, an orange
        vinyl chair and a window where among sloping telephone
        wires, the top branches of a bare tree can be seen.

                              MS. ROBINSON (CONT'D)
                    These are just the bare essentials, of
                    course. Once you move in, you can dress
                    it up anyway you want.
                         (poking her head through the
                          courtesy curtain)
                    Mr. Sperry? You want to meet your new
                    neighbor? Mr. Savage?

        After a moment, she pulls the curtain open to expose MR.
        SPERRY, 80, in a hospital gown reading a large print
        Agatha Christie mystery. He greets the family with a
        stiff wave and a crooked smile.

                              MR. SPERRY
                    Hi there.

An odd suspended moment as everyone looks at the old man in the bed. And then, just like that, Ms. Robinson closes the curtain. Show's over.

>   MS. ROBINSON
>   I'll leave you alone to look around and
>   get yourselves together.
>   (low to Jon)
>   I need you to sign some papers. I'll
>   send someone in to get him ready for bed.

74   **LATER --**   74

Wendy is putting Lenny's clothes into a bureau. An aide enters -- JIMMY, 30, a skinny, handsome Nigerian guy with dreadlocks.

>   JIMMY
>   (Nigerian accent)
>   Hi.

>   WENDY
>   Hi.

>   JIMMY
>   You're gonna need to write down his name
>   on all his things so nothing gets lost.
>   You like red or green?

Jimmy produces TWO LAUNDRY MARKERS. She reaches for the red one.

>   JIMMY (CONT'D)
>   (to Lenny)
>   Good evening sir, I'm Jimmy.

>   LENNY
>   Leonard Savage.

>   JIMMY
>   Good to meet you.

>   LENNY
>   Ditto.

>   JIMMY
>   (to Wendy)
>   Make sure to include B-26, the room
>   number. Lemme show you.

Jimmy steps up to the bureau, takes one of Lenny's t-shirts and writes on the inside collar: *L. Savage. B-26.* Then, with a flourish he draws a silly smiley face. Wendy is charmed. IN THE MIRROR ABOVE THE BUREAU she watches

Jimmy talk to Lenny as she begins to mark Lenny's shirts.

> JIMMY (CONT'D)
> You ready for a good night's sleep?
> Gimme your arms up in the air. Come on.
> Up. Up like you're under arrest.

Lenny lifts his arms stiffly.

> JIMMY (CONT'D)
> Good man. You ever done time, Mr.
> Savage?

Lenny laughs. Jimmy pulls his shirt off over his head.

75   **THE HALLWAY OUTSIDE LENNY'S ROOM - LATER**   75

Mrs. Robinson is giving Jon and Wendy final words of advice.

> MS. ROBINSON
> (hushed voice)
> It's a good idea not to make too big of a
> thing when you leave for the first time.
> Just go real casual. No big good-byes.
> You don't want to get him agitated before
> he adjusts and settles into his new home.

76   **BACK IN THE ROOM --**   76

Wendy and Jon pull on their coats. Lenny watches them
from bed.

> JON
> So everything okay, Dad?

> LENNY
> Not bad.

> JON
> Okay then we'll see you tomorrow.

> WENDY
> Good night Dad.

Jon stands by as Wendy bends down and kisses her father
good night. They head toward the door.

> LENNY
> Hey --

Wendy and Jon stop and turn around, expecting the worst.

> JON
> What, Dad?

LENNY
Don't forget to tip the girl on the way out.
They expect it in a nice hotel like this.

77   **INT. HALLWAY - CONTINUOUS**   77

Jon and Wendy walk quickly and silently toward the exit.

78   **EXT. NURSING HOME PARKING LOT - NIGHT**   78

The heavy door flies open and Wendy and Jon hurl
themselves from the building and crunch across the
parking lot. Breath plumes out of their mouths like
smoke. It's freezing cold.

Halfway across the lot, Wendy stumbles to a halt and
ERUPTS into a fit of tears.

JON
What, Wen?

Through heaving sobs --

WENDY
He didn't even -- know -- where -- we
were taking him.

JON
He still doesn't know. He doesn't know
where he is.

WENDY
We're horrible, horrible, horrible --
people, Jon. Horrible, horrible.

79   **EXT. JON'S HOUSE - NIGHT**   79

The car pulls up.

80   **INT. FOYER/LIVING ROOM - NIGHT**   80

The door opens and Jon and Wendy shuffle into the
darkened foyer. Jon flips on the LIGHTS. Wendy looks
around.

HER POV OF THE LIVING ROOM --
PILES of BOOKS, NEWSPAPERS and MAGAZINES. Heaps of hand
labeled VIDEO AND AUDIO TAPES stacked all around the TV.

                    WENDY
          It looks like the Unibomber lives here.

                    JON
          Yeah, well I've been doing a lot of
          research for the book. The couch is
          actually pretty comfortable.

                    WENDY
          Great... Where is it?

Wendy watches as Jon removes stacks of books that nearly bury
the couch. She joins him and starts to move books as well.

                    JON
          Those need to go over here, actually.

Jon takes the books from Wendy and puts them in a
specific place. When Jon turns around, he discovers that
Wendy is lifting more books from the couch.

                    JON (CONT'D)
              (taking books from her)
          It doesn't look like it, I know, but
          there's actually a system to all of this.

                    WENDY
              (with raised hands)
          Ooooh-kay.

Wendy moves out of the way and watches as her brother
obsessively re-organizing the books.

81   **INT. JON'S BEDROOM - NIGHT**   81

Wendy flips on a light and enters. She takes A PILLOW
from Jon's unmade bed, then notices a PRESCRIPTION PILL
BOTTLE on his nightstand. She picks up the bottle,
yelling downstairs --

                    WENDY
          Jon, what's Zocor?

                    JON (O.S.)
          Get out of my room, Wendy.

                    WENDY
          Is that for depression?

                    JON (O.S.)
          It's for cholesterol.

                              WENDY
                    You have high cholesterol?

                              JON (O.S.)
                    Yes!

Now Wendy notices A SHOPPING BAG full of MAIL AND
BROCHURES. She kneels down to take a closer look.

                              WENDY
                    Is this all your nursing home research?

                              JON
                    Wendy!

82   **INT. LIVING ROOM - LATER**   82

The couch has been made, but Jon is still organizing his
books, apparently unable to stop. Wendy shuffles in,
carrying the pillow and the shopping bag she found
upstairs. She tosses the pillow on the couch and sits down
to dig through the bag.

                              WENDY
                    Most of these aren't even open.

                              JON
                    I got on some list, they just keep
                    coming.

Wendy pulls out a large, full-color brochure and begins
to leaf through it.

                              WENDY
                    Hill Haven. This looks nice.

                              JON
                    It's in Vermont. I really wish you
                    hadn't brought that down.

Wendy stuffs the brochure back into the bag and climbs
under the blanket. She squirms around uncomfortably,
then digs under the cushions and pulls out a A CRUSHED
PAPERBACK.

                              WENDY
                    Jon.

Jon looks up. Wendy holds the book out to him.

                              JON
                    What is it?

                         WENDY
                      (pointedly)
                 "Theater of the Absurd."

Jon retrieves the book, puts it in its proper place and
continues to hover over his piles.

                         WENDY (CONT'D)
                 Are you going to stop?

                         JON
                 Yeah, yeah, sorry.

Jon begins SWITCHING OFF the lights. As he does, he
notices his sister's troubled expression.

                         JON (CONT'D)
                 We're doing the right thing, Wen. We're
                 taking better care of the old man than he
                 ever did of us.

                         WENDY
                      (not sure)
                 I know.

                         JON
                      (climbing the stairs)
                 Goodnight.

                         WENDY
                 'night.

A RADIATOR HISSES as Wendy lies in the dark with her eyes
wide open. A note of MUSIC, then --

                         NARRATOR (PRE-LAP)
                 We know that this is one of the toughest
                 decisions of your life...

                                        DISSOLVE TO:

IMAGES OF CRASHING SURF on a TV.

                         NARRATOR (CONT'D)
                 What to do when the parent who took care
                 of you can no longer take care of
                 themself.

REVERSE ANGLE --

Wendy sits in the dark watching a PROMOTIONAL VIDEOTAPE
for GREENHILL MANOR -- a luxury nursing home. She's
eating a bowl of cereal and the floor around her is
covered in nursing home brochures.

NARRATOR (CONT'D)
We know how hard this can be, that's why
here at Greenhill Manor we are committed
to providing the highest quality of care
to our residents...

The CAMERA MOVES IN ON WENDY as she watches, transfixed.

ON T.V.: images of A BEAUTIFULLY LANDSCAPED ESTATE that
looks more like a New England Prep school than a nursing
home. Words appear and disappear over the images. Words
like: *Commitment. Community. Compassion.* SENTIMENTAL
MUSIC plays over gauzy photos of HAPPY SENIORS being
attended to by a caring STAFF.

83   **EXT. JON'S HOUSE - DAY**   83

From inside the car -- AN ICE AND SNOW PACKED WINDSHIELD.
A SCRAPER appears and pushes the snow away to reveal Jon
on the other side. His breath is visible as he scrapes.
Wendy sits inside and watches.

The camera MOVES TOWARD the windshield, past Wendy,
through the hole Jon has created, past Jon, past the tops
of the trees and into --

83A   **THE WINTER SKY --**   83A
ORCHESTRAL MUSIC SWELLS, a ghostly black and white FRED
ASTAIRE appears and begins to SING, as though performing
for us from the great beyond.

FRED ASTAIRE
Heaven. I'm in heaven. And my heart
beats so that I can hardly speak...

TILT DOWN to reveal --

84   **EXT. VALLEY VIEW - DAY**   84

It looks particularly bleak on this snowy winter day.

85   **OMITTED**   85

86   **INT. VALLEY VIEW - DAY**   86

The music continues, but now it emanates from a BOOMBOX,
suddenly sounding thin and tinny.

A ROOMFUL OF RESIDENTS with their arms over their heads
move in SLOW MOTION in rhythm to the song.

They're taking part in an exercise class overseen by A
PHYSICAL THERAPIST. Lenny is among them, skeptical, but
playing along.

87   **INT. VALLEY VIEW - OFFICE - DAY**   87

Wendy and Jon sit across from an ADMINISTRATOR. Fred
Astaire can be heard in the distance.

>   ADMINISTRATOR
>   (referring to a file)
>   Well, it looks like all his Medicaid is
>   squared away. And as far as his advance
>   directive --

The Administrator pops a pen in her mouth, holding it
between her teeth as she leafs through some papers.

>   WENDY
>   Hey, I take that.

The administrator looks up.

>   WENDY (CONT'D)
>   (pointing)
>   On your pen.

The administrator looks at her pen. It is imprinted with
an ad for *Xanax*.

>   WENDY (CONT'D)
>   For anxiety. Not all the time. Just
>   when I need it.

The administrator smiles vaguely and returns to her work.
Jon looks at his sister sideways.

>   ADMINISTRATOR
>   So here's the Health Care Proxy we talked
>   about and the Living Will material.
>   We'll need these signed both by you and
>   your father.

She holds the papers over the desk. Jon and Wendy both
reach for them, but the administrator hands them to Jon.
Wendy feels slighted.

>   ADMINISTRATOR (CONT'D)
>   The only other thing missing is the
>   paperwork regarding funeral arrangements.
>   We'll need to know about your father's
>   burial or cremation plans.

Wendy and Jon stare at her, taken aback.

88   **OMITTED**   88

89   **INT. DINER - DAY**   89

The Savages sit in a booth. Jon is holding A HEARING AID
between two fingers showing it to his father like it's an
exotic bug.

                    JON
          You see Dad, if you switch this little
          thing here you can change the volume and
          you can turn it off.

Jon hands the hearing aid to Lenny. Lenny puts it in his
ear.

                    JON (CONT'D)
          How's that? Is it a good level?

                    LENNY
          Yeah.

An awkward pause. Wendy and Jon exchange nervous looks.

                    JON
          Uh, Dad we need to talk about a couple of
          things.

                    LENNY
          Okay.

                    WENDY
          We don't want you to take it in the wrong
          way.

                    JON
          It's just some questions that'll make
          everything easier in the long run.

Lenny nods reasonably. Wendy nervously begins --

                    WENDY
          Okay, if um, in the event that something
          happens, how would you, um, you know,
          want us to, uh--

                    JON
          Dad, suppose you were in a coma?

                    WENDY
          Jon!

                    JON
Would you want a breathing machine to
keep you alive?

                    LENNY
What kind of question is that?

                    JON
It's a question that we should know the
answer to -- in case.

                    LENNY
In case what?

                    JON
In case something happens.

                    WENDY
          (to Lenny)
But nothing's happening right now.
Nothing new.

                    JON
It's just procedure. Something they want
for their records.

                    LENNY
Who?

                    WENDY
The people that run the place. The
Valley View.

                    LENNY
What the hell kind of hotel is it?

                    JON
It's not a hotel, Dad. It's a nursing
home.

A stunned silence. Lenny's eyes drift to a spot on the
ground and stay focused there. Jon immediately regrets
having been so direct. Wendy glares at him. After a
long pause --

                    LENNY
          (mumbling)
Unplug me.

                    JON
What?

                    LENNY
               (loud and clear)
          Pull the plug.

Nearby CUSTOMERS look in their direction. Jon and Wendy
lower their voices.

                    JON
          Okay, Dad. So, now, once we unplug
          you...

                    LENNY
          I'm dead.

                    JON
          Right. And then we...

                    LENNY
          What?

                    JON
          What do we do with you?

Lenny looks at both his children and then he breaks into
a fit of wheezing laughter.

                    LENNY
               (talking through laughter)
          You bury me. What're you a bunch of
          idiots? You bury me.

Lenny continues laughing. Unnerved by his outburst,
Wendy and Jon stare silently at their father, unsure
whether to laugh or cry.

90   **INT. JON'S HOUSE - FOYER - NIGHT**   90

The front door opens. Wendy steps into the darkened house
and switches on a LIGHT. She turns around, startled to
discover --

A WOMAN IN A BATHROBE, sitting in the dimly lit living
room, holding a glass of whiskey.

                    WENDY
          Jesus!

                    KASIA
               (Eastern European accent)
          Sorry to scare you.

                    WENDY
          That's okay.

                    KASIA
          Jon didn't tell you?

                    WENDY
          What?

                    KASIA
          That I was coming. Typical.

Just then, Jon appears at the front door, carrying a BIG
LAUNDRY BAG.

                    KASIA (CONT'D)
               (to Jon)
          You just gave your sister heart attack.
          She didn't expect to find Polish woman in
          her brother's home.

                    JON
               (to Wendy)
          I told you.

                    WENDY
          No you didn't.

                    JON
          Yes I did. I'm taking Kash to the
          airport in the morning. Early flight.

Jon hoists the bag over his shoulder and heads upstairs.

                    KASIA
          Very early. We should leave by 6:30 at
          latest.

                    JON (OS)
          Okay.

Kasia looks at Wendy, shrugs sadly and gets up.

                    KASIA
          It's back to Krakow for Kasia.

                    WENDY
          Yeah, Jon told me. I'm sorry.

Kasia walks to the stairs, pausing at the bottom.

                    KASIA
          Your brother won't marry me, but when I
          cook him eggs, he cries.
               (a big sigh)
          I should take cab to airport like self-
          respecting feminist woman, but here I am.

Kasia climbs the stairs.

91   **INT. KITCHEN - MORNING**   91

Eggs fry on the stove. Kasia tends to them with a spatula.

LATER -- Wendy, Jon and Kasia eat silently. After a
moment, the sound of SNIFFLES. Wendy looks up from her
plate and sees -- Jon tearing up with appreciation as he
chews. Wendy and Kasia exchange a look.

92   **EXT. JON'S HOUSE - DAY**   92

The COROLLA IDLES out front. Kasia climbs in as Jon loads
the trunk with suitcases. Wendy stands in the doorway
wearing a coat over her pajamas as she waves goodbye.

93   **INT. UNIVERSITY GYM - TENNIS COURT - NIGHT**   93

Wendy and Jon, dressed in old T-shirts and Converse sneakers,
chase the ball with their rackets.

                         WENDY
             How'd it go at the airport?

                         JON
             Fine.

                         WENDY
             Was it emotional?

                         JON
             No. Not really.

                         WENDY
             She loves you.

                         JON
             Yeah, well... there are practical
             considerations that love has nothing to
             do with.

Wendy races after the ball and lobs it over the net.

                         WENDY
             Like what?

Her return goes way out of bounds. Jon shuffles across
the court to retrieve the wayward ball.

                              JON
          Wendy, do you have any idea how many
          Comp-Lit-Critical Theory PhDs there are
          running around this country looking for work?
          Even if Kasia and I did get married and she
          stayed, she could end up teaching at some
          university that's farther away from here than
          Poland... and then we wouldn't be together
          either. See what I'm saying?

Wendy makes a comically confused face.

                              WENDY
          You're an idiot.

                              JON
          Can we just play the game?

                              WENDY
          Fine.

Jon hits the ball to Wendy. She returns it.

                              WENDY (CONT'D)
          I got us an interview.

                              JON
          For what?

                              WENDY
          A really nice alternative to the Valley
          View.

                              JON
                    (irritated)
          We just got him in there!

                              WENDY
          Can you hold your judgements until you
          see this place. It's beautiful. It's
          called Greenhill Manor.

                              JON
          Sounds like an insane asylum.

With a loud grunt, Jon hits an angry back-handed return,
then suddenly drops his racket, grips the side of his
neck and grimaces in pain...

                              JON (CONT'D)
          Oww!

                              WENDY
          Are you okay?

                    JON
                 (writhing)
        No, I am not okay!

                    WENDY
        Are you having a heart attack?

                    JON
        No, Wendy I am not having a heart attack!
                 (more pain)
        Fuck!

94   **INT. KITCHEN - NIGHT**   94

Wendy stands at the sink filling up a medical-looking
VINYL BAG with water.

                    WENDY
                 (calling off-screen)
        How much do I fill it up?

                    JON (OS)
        Twenty pounds.

Wendy looks at the bag and sees MEASURING MARKS with
numbers indicating poundage. She fills it to TWENTY.

95   **THE FOYER --**   95

Wendy enters carrying the unwieldy bag of water. She arrives
before Jon who stands against the front door shirtless and
wearing a strange HARNESS CONTRAPTION wrapped underneath his
chin and around his head. Cords and pulleys attached to it
lead to a bracket that is hooked over the top of the door.
The overall effect is not unlike that of a man preparing to
hang himself.

                    WENDY
        What do I do with it?

                    JON
                 (holding a rod)
        Hook it to this.

Wendy attaches the water bag to the apparatus and then steps
back to observe the fully assembled contraption. The sight
of Jon hanging there makes Wendy laugh. This makes Jon
start to laugh, but the laughing pains him further.

                    JON (CONT'D)
        Ow! Don't laugh.
                 (Wendy laughs more)
        It's not funny.

> WENDY
> What's it supposed to do?

> JON
> Relieve pressure. I have to stay like
> this for thirty minutes.

Wendy looks at her brother and, unable to contain
herself, she lets out another round of laughter.

> JON (CONT'D)
> Wendy! Give me my mail.

Wendy hands him a pile of mail from a nearby table. He sifts
through it and stops when he comes to A BUBBLE ENVELOPE.

> JON (CONT'D)
> This is for you.
> (re: the return address)
> Who's Larry Mendelsohn?

Wendy grabs it from him.

> WENDY
> (defensive)
> A friend... forwarding me my mail.

Jon narrows his eyes.

> JON
> Is that the married guy?

Wendy heads toward the kitchen, leaving her brother
pinned to the door.

> WENDY
> I'm starving. You want something to eat?

> JON
> I thought you stopped seeing that creep.

> WENDY (OS)
> How about tuna melts?

96   **INT. KITCHEN - NIGHT**   96

TWO OPEN FACED TUNA MELTS glow in an ANCIENT TOASTER OVEN.
Wendy stands at the counter quickly sorting through her mail
and stops when she gets to A CERTAIN ENVELOPE. Turning it
over in her hands, she carefully opens it and pulls out the
letter.

CLOSE ON WENDY reading with great concentration. She is deeply engrossed and still for a long moment, then her eyes widen and her hand flutters to her mouth. She can't believe what she is reading. It's good news, but there seems to be a little hesitation as well. Then -- DING!!! -- the toaster oven bell startles her.

97   **INT. FOYER - NIGHT**   97

Wendy enters, carrying her mail along with the TUNA MELTS.

                    WENDY
               (handing one to Jon)
          Here you go.

                    JON
          Mmm. Thanks.

Jon takes the tuna melt and cautiously nibbles a corner. Wendy perches on the arm of a chair.

                    JON (CONT'D)
          I need you to spend Thanksgiving with Dad.

                    WENDY
          We're not going to do it together?

                    JON
          It's my only time to get away for research.

                    WENDY
          Well, I have things I have to do, too.

                    JON
               (with a mouth full of tuna)
          Like what?

                    WENDY
          Like my life for instance in New York City.

                    JON
          Well, maybe it's time to stop being so
          self involved and think about somebody
          else's life for a change.

                    WENDY
          Oh, like you who can't put his book aside
          for one minute while dad dies.

                    JON
I have got to get this thing finished,
Wendy. My editor thinks it's a good time
for it.

                    WENDY
Yeah, I heard everyone's really itching
for a book about Bertolt Brecht this
holiday season.

                    JON
Wendy I'm working!

Wendy is hurt. Tears well up against her will.

                    WENDY
          (tiny)
I'm working.

                    JON
I know you are. I'm sorry. I'm sorry.
I'm sorry. It's just -- I got a lot
riding on this book. And your life is
much more portable than mine.

                    WENDY
What's that supposed to mean? Like a
toilet? Like a Porta-Potty?

                    JON
No. I'm just saying, you don't have a
job job. I do. I have obligations.
You're... freelance. Couldn't you just
hook up with a temp agency down here?

Wendy is shaky. There is a warble in her voice.

                    WENDY
Um -- actually -- Jon, I am being funded,
right now... to work on my plays. And
maybe that sounds a little -- self-
involved -- but I also have an obligation
to a prestigious foundation that has put
a lot of faith in me -- and frankly, has
given me a hell of a lot more support
than he ever has.

A pause. Jon is quietly stunned.

                    JON
You got it?

                    WENDY
What?

                    JON
          The Guggenheim?

Wendy sniffs back her tears and gets control of herself,
but there is something measured about her response.

                    WENDY
          Yeah.

                    JON
          Really?

                    WENDY
          Yeah, really. Why do you sound so
          surprised?

                    JON
          I'm not. It's just a really hard thing
          to get is all. I've applied a half a
          dozen times and I never got one.

                    WENDY
          Well, I did. And so did two hundred-
          something other people who are considered
          -- promising in their field or whatever.
          Why can't you just be happy for me?

                    JON
          I am. I am. It's great.
               (bewildered)
          They must have like a whole different set
          of criteria for playwrights.

                    WENDY
          They like my work, Jon. They think I'm
          good. Is that so hard for you to believe?

                    Jon
          I believe it. I just can't believe
          you've been keeping it a secret.

                    WENDY
          I just found out.

                    JON
          Just now?

Wendy nods yes and gestures to the mail in her hand.

                    JON (CONT'D)
          Oh my god, that's amazing. It's really
          great, Wen. I'm really proud of you...

                    WENDY
          You are?

                    JON
          Yeah. It's amazing. It's major. Maybe
          this is your time, Wen. Your year. Look,
          how about we both work here and ride out the
          holidays together and get lots of writing
          done. It'll be fun. We can inspire each
          other. Our own little writers' colony.

After a moment, Wendy nods yes.

                    JON (CONT'D)
          I'm really proud of you, Wen.

98   **INT. FOYER - MORNING**   98

Jon walks down the stairs wearing a FOAM NECK BRACE.
Once in the foyer, he stiffly pulls on his coat, grabs
his satchel and turns around to find --

A BULGING ENVELOPE Scotch-taped to the front door. A
note on it says: *Jon, these might help. Love, Wen.*

Jon removes a prescription pill bottle from the envelope.
The label reads: *Doris Metzger -- Percocet.*

99   **INT. LIVING ROOM - MORNING**   99

Wendy sleeps on the couch. Jon appears over her as he
examines the vial.

                    JON
          Do they work?

Wendy peels open her eyes and nods yes. Jon opens the
vial, spills a pill in his hand, considers it for a
moment and swigs back with a nearby bottle of water. He
places the vial on the coffee table.

                    WENDY
          Don't forget that thing tonight.

Jon gives her a pained look.

                    WENDY (CONT'D)
          You promised.

Jon nods in agreement and leaves. Upon hearing the SOUND
OF THE FRONT DOOR CLOSING, Wendy notices the bottle of
Percocet Jon left behind and thinks, "Why not?" She
smiles dreamily and reaches for the bottle.

A99   LATER --   A99

A NEEDLE IS PLACED ON AN ALBUM. The Kinks play from the
turntable. Wendy does a sexy, utterly private Percocet-
induced dance in the living room.

100   **INT./EXT. JON'S CAR - DAY - MOVING**   100

THROUGH THE WINDSHIELD, Jon watches --
Traffic lights that hang from wires floating overhead
against the dark winter sky.

As Jon drives, he begins to appreciate the understated
beauty of Buffalo as it blurs by. Boy, that Percocet
works fast!

After a while, Jon digs around in his GLOVE COMPARTMENT.
He produces an ANCIENT CASSETTE and inserts it into his
TAPE DECK. It's a scratchy old recording of "3 Penny
Opera." His foam collar does not prevent him from
singing along vigorously in German.

101   **INT. JON'S BATHROOM - DAY**   101

Wendy is in the tub, talking on the phone. ANOTHER ALBUM
plays on the stereo downstairs. She holds her legs in
the air, admiring her chipped nail-polished toes.

                    WENDY
                 (intimate)
          You're in my apartment?

102   **INT. WENDY'S APARTMENT - DAY**   102

Larry lounges on the bed. INTERCUT.

                    LARRY (ON PHONE)
          I'm on your bed with Marley. She's got
          one of your t-shirts.
                 (a deep inhale)
          Mmmm. It smells like you. Like lavender
          and sweat. Genghis is here, too. I'm
          totally getting a hard-on.

                    WENDY
Will you please --

                    LARRY
Sorry.

                    WENDY
How's Genghis?

                    LARRY
She's good. You wanna hear her?

                    WENDY
Yeah.

                    LARRY
C'mere honey. C'mon...

Larry holds the phone up to Genghis. She MEOWS.

                    WENDY
          (into phone, to cat)
Hello beast. Hello Bunny.

                    LARRY
See, she misses you.

                    WENDY
Are you giving her her medication?

                    LARRY
          (he can't remember)
Yep.

                    WENDY
Did you water my plant?

Larry suddenly glances over at the visibly DEHYDRATED FICUS.

                    LARRY
Yep. It's doing good.
          (pause)
When are you coming back?

                    WENDY
After the holidays. Thanks for sending
me my mail.

                    LARRY
No problem... Wen?

                    WENDY
Yeah?

                    LARRY
          I'm leaving town next week for a week.
          I won't be able to take care of Genghis.

                    WENDY
          Where are you going?

                    LARRY
          Toronto... To visit Annie's family.

Wendy slides her legs into the tub and is silent.

                    LARRY (CONT'D)
          It's her parents' twenty-fifth
          anniversary.

Wendy's eyes suddenly well-up with tears as she stares at
the ceiling.

                    LARRY (CONT'D)
          Wendy?... Wendy?

                    WENDY
          Didya lose your hard-on?

                    LARRY
          Wendy, c'mon. How about I drive up and
          bring Genghis? We can spend the
          afternoon together. It'll be fun.
                    (Wendy doesn't answer)
          I know it's not the greatest offer in the
          world, but it's something. I'd love to
          be more of a support, but you know my
          situation...

Wendy continues to stare up at the ceiling.

103   **INT. YMCA - FUNCTION ROOM - NIGHT**   103

A female VOLUNTEER COUNSELOR in a colorful sweater
conducts a support group. On a blackboard behind her it
says: "Healing Through Reminiscence."

                    COUNSELOR
          Now if we could all look at the second
          page of the blue handouts, you'll see a
          section called "Creating Special
          Moments."

Twenty middle-aged FAMILY CARE-GIVERS, sit on folding
chairs flipping through PHOTO-COPIED HANDOUTS.

> COUNSELOR (CONT'D)
> If you're ever at a loss for what to do
> on a visiting day with your elder, this
> list will come in very handy.

The DOOR in the back opens to reveal Wendy and Jon.

> COUNSELOR (CONT'D)
> (to Wendy and Jon)
> Hello.

The entire room turns to look at them. They smile
awkwardly.

> COUNSELOR (CONT'D)
> Are you here for the support group?
> (Wendy and Jon vaguely nod)
> You have a family member with dementia?
> (they nod again)
> Well, you're in the right place. Come on
> in.

The audience begins to APPLAUD for them.

> COUNSELOR (CONT'D)
> Jeanine, could you get them a couple of
> packets.

JEANINE, another volunteer, setting out COOKIES and JUICE
hands Wendy and Jon a packet.

> COUNSELOR (CONT'D)
> There's plenty of room up front.

Wendy and Jon move a few steps inside the room but remain
standing near the door.

> COUNSELOR (CONT'D)
> We're not gonna hurt you. You've
> probably been hurt enough already.

The audience CLAPS and CHUCKLES in agreement. Wendy and
Jon are unnerved by the cultish group dynamic.

> COUNSELOR (CONT'D)
> (addressing the group again)
> We're talking about activities you can
> share with your confused elder on
> visiting days. Now, I culled this list
> from a terrific book--

She reaches into a BIG CANVAS BAG, pulls out "Eldercare
for Dummies." The audience giggles.

                    COUNSELOR (CONT'D)
You laugh, but I love this series.
          (thumbing through pages)
When my mother was diagnosed with
Parkinson's, this was my bible. Consider
it assigned reading.

Wendy notices that the table next to them is laid out
with sweets. She takes a couple of napkins and helps
herself to cookies, offering some to Jon.

                    COUNSELOR
Okay, so.
         (reading from book)
"Creating Special Moments." Number One:
Ask your elder about the old days.
         (in her own words)
Now, that may seem a little obvious, but
when you're dealing with dementia you
gotta work extra hard at this. You can't
just sit on the side of the bed asking
questions. You've got to bring things in
to help stimulate their memories. Old
movies can be a terrific --

Distracted, she looks toward the back of the room.

                    COUNSELOR (CONT'D)
Excuse me --

Wendy and Jon turn around, their mouths stuffed with
food.

                    COUNSELOR (CONT'D)
We haven't served refreshments yet.

The whole room looks at them, indignant.

104   **OMITTED**   104

105   **INT. LOUNGE - NIGHT**   105

Jon and Wendy have "signed out" the room for the evening
to show a movie. A hand-lettered sign is on display:

                  CLASSIC MOVIE NIGHT
            PRESENTED BY LEONARD SAVAGE
                    7:30 PM
                COME ONE, COME ALL!

SCHMALTZY MELODRAMATIC MUSIC PLAYS. A DOZEN OR SO
RESIDENTS are watching BLACK AND WHITE IMAGES flicker on
the screen.

Jon and Wendy sit on either side of Lenny, who is
transfixed by what he sees.

Images of Manhattan's Lower East Side in the 1920's are
reflected in Lenny's EYEGLASSES.

> JON
> (whispering)
> Is that your neighborhood, Dad?

> LENNY
> (mumbling)
> Yep. They got that right.

Some STAFF stand in the back of the room -- KITCHEN
WORKERS and a couple of NURSES.

ON SCREEN -- a MOTHER cooks in a tenement kitchen.

> LENNY (CONT'D)
> There she is.

> JON & WENDY
> Who?

> LENNY
> (irritated, but quiet)
> You see her. She's cooking dinner for
> me.

ON SCREEN -- A FATHER FIGURE enters.

> LENNY (CONT'D)
> There's the bastard.

> JON
> That's the father.

> LENNY
> (yelling at the screen)
> Bastard!

MR. MCGILL, a perpetually disgruntled resident, asserts
himself.

> MR. MCGILL
> Shut up up there.

> LENNY
> You shut yourself up. It's my night.

Lenny pushes himself up and gestures at the screen.

                    LENNY (CONT'D)
               (yelling)
          He smacks me around!

                    JON
          Dad. It's okay. Sit down.

Lenny remains standing, staring at the screen. MADELINE,
another resident, speaks up.

                    MADELINE
          You're in the way of the program.

More PROTESTS from other residents follow, but Lenny is
oblivious.

                    MR. MCGILL
          Down in front!

                    NURSE
          Mr. Savage --

                    WENDY
          Jon, he's got to sit down.

Lenny, suddenly realizing that he's creating a scene,
calms down. Jon helps him back in his chair.

                    JON
          Come on, Dad.

LATER --

It's quieter now. The audience is under the spell of the
movie.

ON SCREEN -- A DANCE PRODUCTION is underway. A WHITE
ENTERTAINER begins to apply BLACK MAKE-UP to his face.

JON watches with academic interest.

WHISPERING comes from the back of the room. Wendy twists
around in her chair to see what's going on.

HER POV -- The STAFF (Haitian, Jamaican, Dominican) are
mumbling to each other.

Wendy sinks low in her seat. She nudges her brother and
gestures for him to take a look. He twists around.

JON'S POV -- More whispering and head shaking from the
staff. Snippets of various dialects can be heard.

ON SCREEN -- Finished with the application of his makeup, the entertainer gives a big white showbiz smile.

106   **INT. VALLEY VIEW - HALLWAY - NIGHT**   106

Wendy and Jon walk down the corridor wearing their coats. Jon holds THE VIDEOTAPE RENTAL in his hands.

> JON
> You can't judge it by today's standards. You have to look at it in a historical context. I just thought Dad would enjoy an old movie.

Wendy and Jon arrive at the ELEVATOR DOORS situated across from THE NURSES STATION, where a small group of NURSES AND AIDES are gathered.

> WENDY & JON
> (aggressively cheerful)
> Goodnight.

As Wendy and Jon wait for the elevator, the group at the nurses station regards them with flat stares.

> WENDY
> (quietly to Jon)
> Thank God we've got that interview tomorrow.

Jon punches the "down" button a few more times.

> JON
> Let's take the stairs.

Jon exits and Wendy follows.

107   **EXT. GREENHILL MANOR NURSING HOME - DAY**   107

We recognize the BEAUTIFULLY LANDSCAPED ESTATE from the video brochure, only now it's live. Under a bright blue winter sky, Wendy pushes Lenny up a path. Jon trails behind.

> WENDY
> They're going to ask you a bunch of questions and you're really going to have to concentrate, Dad. It's important.

> LENNY
> Oh-kay.

The family disappears inside the imposing MAIN BUILDING.

108   **INT. WAITING AREA - DAY**   108

In a strange variation on the college admissions process,
Lenny, Wendy and Jon sit among other ELDERLY PEOPLE and
their ADULT CHILDREN, also waiting to be interviewed.

Jon reads a brochure while Wendy surreptitiously sizes up
the competition. She digs a SMALL PACKET from her purse,
and shakes a few PILLS into the palm of her hand.

                    WENDY
          Dad, open your mouth.

Wendy puts the pills in Lenny's mouth and holds a water
bottle to his lips.

                    JON
          What is that?

                    WENDY
          Ginkoa-Biloba. Boosts brain functions.
               (offering him a packet)
          You want some?
               (off his dismissive look)
          It's ancient, Jon. I'm not making it up.
               (he's still skeptical)
          Fine. Do what you want.

Jon watches as she tosses the packet back into her purse
and digs around for something else. She uncovers an
PRESCRIPTION BOTTLE and dispenses two pills into her hand.

                    JON
          It's like a drugstore in there.

Wendy ignores him and pops the pills into her mouth.

                    JON (CONT'D)
          What're those?

                    WENDY
               (pills on tongue)
          Anthidaprethens. You thoud thry them.

                    JON
          I'm not depressed.

                    WENDY
          Oh, pleethe.

Wendy swigs back the pills.

                              WOMAN (O.S.)
                    You must be the Savages.

Wendy and Jon turn to see ROZ LANDRESS (50) an ADMISSIONS
COUNSELOR with a FILE tucked under her arm.

109   **INT. INTERVIEW ROOM - DAY**   109

Wendy, Jon and Roz sit around a Formica table.

                              ROZ
                    Mr. Savage, I'm going to ask you a few
                    questions --

Loudly proclaiming in a stiff formal style --

                              LENNY
                    MY NAME IS LEONARD MICHAEL JOSEPH SAVAGE.

Roz smiles kindly.

                              ROZ
                    Okay...

Lenny glances over his shoulder to Wendy and Jon as if to
say, "This test is gonna be a cinch."

                              ROZ (CONT'D)
                    Lenny can you tell me what season we're
                    in?

                              LENNY
                    Cold!

Everyone laughs lightly.

                              ROZ
                    And the season is?

                              LENNY
                    Winter. What d'ya think?

                              ROZ
                    And what is the date today?

                              LENNY
                    November. I don't know the day...

                              ROZ
                    Okay. Can you tell me where we are?
                         (pause)
                    What city are we in?

Lenny thinks for a moment. He looks lost. And then,
like a boss dictating to his secretary, he gestures to
her paper.

                    LENNY
          Put down 'East Coast.'

Roz smiles and writes something down. While her head is
lowered, Wendy taps her father's elbow and mouths --
"Buffalo."

Lenny takes a moment, then confidently announces --

                    LENNY (CONT'D)
          Boston!

Roz looks up.

                    LENNY (CONT'D)
               (loud, with conviction)
          Boston, Mass.

Jon widens his eyes and looks at his sister in disbelief.
Roz sees this exchange.

                    ROZ
          You can't help him, Ms. Savage. He has
          to be able to answer the questions
          himself.

                    WENDY
          It's just I know he knows where we are --

                    JON
          Wendy!

                    WENDY
          What? He does.

                    JON
          She's conducting a test!

                    WENDY
          I know. I'm not an idiot, Jon --

                    LENNY
               (loud, quavering)
          LET HER ASK ME THE GODDAMN QUESTIONS!

Lenny's whole body seems to shake and bob from the
exertion. Everyone is silenced.

110   **EXT. GREENHILL MANOR NURSING HOME - DAY**   110

Jon pushes Lenny away from the building. Wendy follows.
From their tense expressions and sideways glances, it's
clear they have a lot to say to each other, but are
somehow managing to hold it. The march to Jon's car is
painfully silent. Then --

CLUNK! Jon closes the passenger door on Lenny and
immediately lays into Wendy.

                    JON
          What did you say to them?

                    WENDY
               (guilty and fast)
          I said he was pretty good except
          sometimes he goes in and out.

                    JON
          In and out? Wendy, the man has dementia!

                    WENDY
          I know, but... they only had beds for
          people that were more independent... and
          I thought if we could just get him in
          there....

Jon notices Lenny peering out from the car and urgently
gestures for Wendy to follow him. He marches several
yards away from the car. Wendy catches up with him.

                    JON
          You're wasting our time on fantasies.

                    WENDY
          She said she'd put him on one of the
          waiting lists. I mean, Jesus, I'm just
          doing it for Dad.

                    JON
          Wendy, Dad is not the one that has a
          problem with the Valley View.

                    WENDY
          I just want to improve Dad's situation.
          Is that a crime?

                    JON
          There is nothing wrong with Dad's
          situation. Dad's situation is fine. But
          he's never going to adjust to it if we
          keep yanking him out of there.
               (MORE)

                    JON (CONT'D)
          Actually, this whole upward mobility
          fixation of yours is counter productive
          and frankly pretty selfish.

                    WENDY
          Selfish?

                    JON
          This thing isn't about Dad, it's about
          you. You and your guilt. That's what
          these places prey upon.

                    WENDY
          I just think it's nicer here.

                    JON
          Of course you do. You're the consumer that
          they want to target. You're the guilty
          demographic. The landscaping, the
          "neighborhoods of care." They're not for
          the residents. They're for the relatives,
          like you and me who don't want to admit
          what is really going on here.

                    WENDY
          Which is...?

He bellows.

                    JON
          People are DYING, Wendy! Right inside
          that beautiful building -- right now!
          It's a fucking HORROR show! And all this
          wellness propaganda and landscaping is
          just trying to obscure the miserable fact
          that people die and death is gaseous and
          gruesome and filled with piss and shit
          and rot and stink!

The FAINT SOUND OF SQUEAKING. Jon and Wendy turn to see --

A WOMAN WHEELING HER FRAIL GRANDMOTHER across the lot.
She is clearly upset by Jon's ranting.

                    WOMAN
               (protectively)
          C'mon Nana.

Wendy and Jon watch the women pass, deeply ashamed of
their display. To make things worse, they notice that
Lenny is peering out at them from the car, bewildered by
what's going on.

                                        FADE OUT

111   **OMITTED**   111

112   **OMITTED**   112

113   **INT. VALLEY VIEW NURSING HOME - DAY**   113

ON THE EVENTS BULLETIN BOARD. A PAPER THANKSGIVING
TURKEY is plucked off and replaced by A PAPER SANTA,
which is STAPLE GUNNED down. The CAMERA PANS to find --

Wendy walking down the hall carrying several shopping
bags from URBAN OUTFITTERS.

114   **INT. LENNY'S ROOM - DUSK**   114

A SERIES OF SHOTS as Wendy decorates the room with:

-- A BEDSIDE LAMP. She CLICKS IT ON and steps back to
admire its cozy amber glow.
-- A LARGE RED VELOUR PILLOW, which she props against the
headboard.
-- A SUPERMARKET PLANT that she finds a spot for on the
windowsill.
--A BRONZE GANESH which she positions next to the plant.

115   LATER --   115

Wendy inserts a plug in the wall and looks up at her most
extravagant purchase -- A LAVA LAMP, glowing ominously on
the bureau.

                        WENDY
                What do you think, Dad?

WIDE --
Night has fallen. Lenny sits on the side of the bed in
his newly decorated room, which is now less nursing home,
more dorm room.

                        LENNY
                (looking at the lava lamp)
                What's it do?

                        WENDY
                Nothing. It's just something to look at.

Lenny nods in bewildered appreciation.

                         YOUNG AIDE (OS)
               How you doing Mr. Savage?

                         LENNY
               Hi ya Jimmy.

Wendy whips around, eager to see Jimmy, but discovers
ANOTHER YOUNG BLACK AIDE entering the room instead.
She's deeply embarrassed by her father's mistake.

                         WENDY
               That's not Jimmy, Dad.

                         LENNY
               The hell are you talking about?

                         WENDY
               It's someone else.
                    (to the aide)
               Sorry, he's kind of...

                         AIDE
                    (unfazed)
               That's alright.
                    (to Lenny)
               It's Howard, Mr. Savage. I'm here to put
               you in bed. Thursday is Jimmy's night
               off.

As Howard begins helping Lenny get ready for bed, Wendy
puts her coat on.

                         WENDY
               I better get going.
                    (kissing him)
               Good night. Dad.

                         LENNY
               Good night.

On her way out, through the curtain --

                         WENDY
               Goodnight, Mr. Sperry.

                         MR. SPERRY (O.S.)
               Goodnight.

Howard tucks Lenny in and SNAPS the bed-rail up. A
MECHANICAL HUM can be heard as Howard lowers the bed into
the sleeping position. Howard SHUTS OFF the new bedside
lamp, then goes to the lava lamp and CLICKS IT OFF as
well. The room is dark.

LENNY
(mumbling)
Leave it on.

HOWARD
Are you sure? Won't keep you up?

LENNY
Yeah, I'm sure.

HOWARD
(turning the lava lamp on)
Alright. There you go. Good night Mr.
Savage.

LENNY
Good night.

Howard leaves. Like a child who is scared of the dark,
Lenny pulls the blankets up to his face, leaving only his
eyes exposed. He looks at the lava lamp for comfort. The
red liquid globs move about hypnotically.

116   **INT. JON'S STUDY - DAY**   116

In his second floor office, Jon types at his computer.
Interrupted by A HONKING HORN, he looks out the window.

JON'S POV --
A CAR idles in the street. Wendy appears, pulling on her
coat as she hurries toward the car.

117   **EXT. STREET - CONTINUOUS**   117

Wendy arrives at the open window of the car. Larry is
inside with Marley, who is overjoyed to see Wendy.

LARRY
Hey, Wen.

WENDY
Hi.

They exchange a simple, unromantic kiss. Marley tries to
climb over Larry and get her share of attention.

LARRY
Whoa, Marley. Take it easy.

WENDY
(rubbing Marley's head)
Yes, honey. You, too. You, too.
(MORE)

                    WENDY (CONT'D)
                (to Larry)
        Where's the beast?

Larry reaches into the foot-well behind the passenger
seat and lifts up a CAT CARRIER. Through the little
caged opening, Genghis can be seen, MEOWING. Wendy pokes
a finger in and wiggles it around.

                    WENDY (CONT'D)
        Hello bundle. Hello beast.
                (to Larry)
        Did you remember her papers?

He holds up an OLD MANILA FILE, which Wendy takes.

                    WENDY (CONT'D)
        Thanks.
                (re: Marley)
        How's she doing?

                    LARRY
        She's... you know, hanging in there.
        Her hind legs are really bothering her.
        But I found this great vet at The
        Animal Hospital. That place on the
        east side. They have her in physical
        therapy. Do you believe it? She hangs
        out in a whirlpool twice a week.

Wendy lets out a tiny laugh.

                    LARRY (CONT'D)
        Get in. We'll take a ride. I've never
        been to Buffalo.

Wendy hesitates.

                    LARRY (CONT'D)
        Let's have some fun. I've missed you.

Wendy thinks for a moment, then turns and yells up to
Jon's second story office window.

                    WENDY
        Jon! Jon!
                (no response)
        JON!

118   **INT./EXT. JON'S OFFICE - SAME TIME**   118

Jon is at the computer again, trying to concentrate, when
BEEP, BEEP! That horn again! He stops working, looks
out the window, then opens it.

                    JON
          What?

                    WENDY
          I'm gonna go out for a minute.

                    JON
          Okay.

                    WENDY
          Um -- This is my friend, Larry.
                    (to Larry)
          This is Jon.

                    LARRY
                    (waving)
          Hi, Jon.

                    JON
                    (unenthused)
          Hi, Larry.

                    LARRY
          Wendy's told me a lot about you.

Jon nods.

                    LARRY (CONT'D)
          I loved your essay on "Mother Courage,"
          by the way. Wendy showed it to me. I
          did a production of it and it was a huge
          help.

Jon smiles stiffly -- he's not buying this flattery.
Wendy takes the hint.

                    WENDY
          I'll see you later.

                    JON
          Okay.

Jon pulls the window closed and disappears from view. As
Wendy walks around to get in the car --

                    LARRY
          He seems really nice.

Wendy climbs in and notices an unhealthy PLANT poking out
of a box in the backseat.

                    WENDY
          Is that my ficus?

STILLS

The Sun City West Dancers

Photo by Mark Fellman

Philip Seymour Hoffman as Jon Savage and Laura Linney as Wendy Savage, as they arrive at Doris Metzger's house in Sun City, Arizona.

Photo by Mark Fellman

Wendy Savage (Laura Linney) and her brother, Jon (Philip Seymour Hoffman), as they bring their father to the nursing home.

Photo by Andrew Schwartz

Wendy (Laura Linney) kisses her father (Philip Bosco) goodnight.   Photo by Andrew Schwartz

Jon (Philip Seymour Hoffman) clearing his living room for his sister (Laura Linney).

Photo by Andrew Schwartz

Movie Night with Leonard Savage: Wendy (Laura Linney), Lenny (Philip Bosco), and Jon (Philip Seymour Hoffman).

Photo by Andrew Schwartz

Laura Linney and Philip Seymour Hoffman on the set.

Philip Bosco and Tamara Jenkins on the set.   Photo by Andrew Schwartz

Tamara Jenkins directing Philip Seymour Hoffman in the snow.

Photo by Andrew Schwartz

Director Tamara Jenkins.

Photo by Andrew Schwartz

The car takes off.

119   **INT. CAR/EXT. BUFFALO - DAY**   119

A quick sight-seeing MONTAGE. Wendy and Larry try to
have fun at various sights. It's not easy. There's not
much to see in Buffalo.

They drive to NIAGARA FALLS. They take pictures with a
DISPOSABLE CAMERA. Marley hobbles along with them,
trying the best she can to be a part of things. They
play in the snow and throw snowballs at each other.
Larry accidently hits Wendy in the eye and she becomes
angry at him.

122   **EXT. NIAGARA FALLS DAYS INN - NIGHT**   122

Larry's car is parked out front.

123   **INT. NIAGARA FALLS DAYS INN - NIGHT**   123

Larry and Wendy are making out. Genghis and Marley have
found spots for themselves, far from the action. Wendy
suddenly pulls away from Larry.

                    LARRY
          What?

                    WENDY
          I don't know... You killed my plant.

                    LARRY
          No, I didn't.

                    WENDY
          Well, it's not thriving. It was thriving
          when I left.

                    LARRY
          I'm sorry.

She heaves an agitated sigh.

                    WENDY
          It's not the plant. The plant is symbolic.

                    LARRY
          Of what?

Wendy looks at him squarely.

                         WENDY
          What do you think?

                         LARRY
          I know this isn't perfect.

                         WENDY
          Not perfect?! Larry, come on. I have an
          M.F.A., for christsakes! I mean, look at
          this. We're in a motel room in Buffalo.
          It's embarrassing. We're a cliche.

                         LARRY
          What cliché?

                         WENDY
          The mid-life crisis cliché.

                         LARRY
          Whose?

                         WENDY
                   (is he that clueless?)
          Yours. You're married. You're cheating.
          You're sleeping with a younger woman.
          Classic.

     Trying to be gentle, but not entirely successful --

                         LARRY
          Uh, Wendy. You're not exactly a younger
          woman.

                         WENDY
          What's that supposed to mean?

                         LARRY
          You're thirty-nine.

                         WENDY
          You're fifty-two.

                         LARRY
          So?

                         WENDY
          So, that makes you older.

                         LARRY
          Yeah, technically. But this is not
          exactly the paradigm of a prototypical
          winter/spring romance. Annie's forty-six.

     Wendy looks at him.

                    LARRY (CONT'D)
          I mean, you're not my little student.
          It's not like we've got "The Blue Angel"
          going on here.

The comment just lands there oddly. Wendy cocks her head to
the side and makes an exaggerated expression of confusion.

                    LARRY (CONT'D)
                    (impatient)
          The professor character in
          "The Blue Angel," the film.

                    WENDY
          I know the movie, Larry.

                    LARRY
          Yeah so, the poor slob has an affair with
          his student and his life is destroyed by
          it. Von Stroheim.

                    WENDY
          Von Sternberg.

                    LARRY
          Whatever. You know what I mean. Marlene
          Dietrich.

                    WENDY
          She's not a student. She's a nightclub
          singer. But there is a Francine Prose
          novel by the same name that is about a
          professor-student relationship --

                    LARRY
          Why do you do this?

                    WENDY
          What?

                    LARRY
          You do it all the time. And on top of
          it, you insult me by telling me I'm the
          one having a mid-life crisis here, when
          you're the one having an affair with a
          married guy instead of seeking real
          intimacy with someone who is available
          for a real commitment. And you know it's
          all about your father.

Wendy is stunned, but keeps going.

                    WENDY
          Hey, I'm just having a normal, healthy
          sex life here. I'm not betraying anyone.

                    LARRY
          Only yourself.

Socked in the stomach and winded --

                    WENDY
          You know, I can't even believe I put up
          with it actually. That I'm even
          participating is so...

                    LARRY
          Sad?

                    WENDY
          What?

                    LARRY
          Nothing.

Wendy stares at Larry, her face tight. A far off RUMBLE
can be heard getting louder and louder. It is the sound
of Wendy's resentment growing.

124   **EXT. VALLEY VIEW - NIGHT**   124

     The RUMBLE continues as Larry's car pulls up and the
     passenger door swings open. Angry and tear-streaked, Wendy
     removes her CAT CARRIER, LITTER BOX and FICUS TREE from his
     car.

     Larry stands by helplessly as she collects everything
     into an awkward bundle and storms off into the facility.

                    LARRY
               (feebly)
          Wendy.

125   **INT. LENNY'S ROOM - CONTINUOUS**   125

     Wendy enters. Lenny watches a Jimmy Cagney movie, WHITE
     HEAT, on T.V. Jon sits in a chair using his laptop. The
     first thing Wendy notices is that the dreaded FLUORESCENT
     LIGHT above Lenny's bed is on. The lamp she bought sits
     on the night table, unlit.

                    WENDY
          Can we not use this horrible light,
          please? It's depressing.

She puts down her load, crosses the room and SWITCHES OFF
the fluorescent light.

                    WENDY (CONT'D)
          I bought you this one, remember?
                    (switching on lamp by bed)
          See how nice it is. It's homey.

No response from Lenny. He concentrates on Jimmy Cagney.
Wendy goes to get the cat carrier.

                    WENDY (CONT'D)
          Dad, I want to show you something.

                    LENNY
          I'm watching a picture.

                    WENDY
          Fine.

Wendy flops down in a chair and thumbs through an old
AARP Magazine called "Modern Maturity."

                    JON
          Wendy?

She turns to her brother who gestures to the cat carrier.

                    JON (CONT'D)
          What's going on with that?

                    WENDY
          It's not going to effect you in any way,
          okay? They said it was perfectly fine to
          have her stay here as long as I can prove
          she's had her shots.

                    JON
          I still don't think it's a good idea.

                    WENDY
          They like animals here, Jon. Apparently,
          they're good for the residents' well-
          being. They reduce stress. So, would
          you please fucking calm down about it!

ON T.V.: The final scene of WHITE HEAT. Cagney on top of
the gas tanks, shoots wildly into a tank and immolates
himself. The End." Wendy switches off the T.V.

                    WENDY (CONT'D)
          Dad, I want you to meet someone.

She lifts up the cat carrier, holding it in front of him.

                    WENDY (CONT'D)
          Look inside.

Lenny tries to lean forward with difficulty.

                    LENNY
          I don't see anything.

                    WENDY
          Here, lemme prop you up.

Wendy puts down the cat carrier and glances around the
room looking for something.

                    WENDY (CONT'D)
          Where's Dad's pillow?

                    JON
          What pillow?

                    WENDY
          The big red one. From Urban Outfitter's.
               (Jon looks blank)
          You saw it. I bought it for him.
               (Jon shrugs)
          Jesus, Jon!

She storms out of the room.

126   **THE NURSE'S STATION DESK - CONTINUOUS**   126

A few NURSING HOME STAFFERS are watching the local news
on a small T.V.

                    WENDY
          Excuse me?

An ATTENDANT looks up. But her attention is split
between Wendy and her program.

                    WENDY (CONT'D)
          My father has a big red pillow I bought
          for him and it's missing from his room.

                    ATTENDANT
          I just started my shift. Try Simone in
          the lounge.

127   **IN THE LOUNGE --**   127

Wendy marches in. Several residents are parked in
wheelchairs staring up at a large T.V.

suspended from the ceiling. An ATTENDANT stands among
them with the remote control flipping through channels
looking for a particular program.

                    WENDY
          Are you Simone?

                    ATTENDANT
          I am.

                    WENDY
          I'm Lenny Savage's daughter in B-26.
          He has a big red pillow I bought for
          him. It's missing.

                    SIMONE
          Did it have his name on it?

                    WENDY
          And his room number.

                    SIMONE
          What's it look like?

                    WENDY
               (flat, sarcastic)
          Big. Red. Pillow.

Simone shakes her head no.

128   **INT. VALLEY VIEW - HALLWAY - NIGHT**   128

An angry Wendy storms back toward her father's room,
stopping in her tracks to turn and look down the opposite
length of the corridor.

WENDY'S POV --
A cluster of residents. Among them -- an OLD WOMAN IN A
WHEELCHAIR, who holds Lenny's RED PILLOW in her lap.

Wendy marches towards the old woman.

                    WENDY
          Excuse me?

No response. The woman is in her own private world. The
CAMERA TILTS down to THE WOMAN'S KNOTTY HANDS, stroking
the pillow like it's a pet.

                    WENDY (CONT'D)
               (louder)
          Excuse me. Ma'am?

The Woman flickers to some vague sense of consciousness and regards Wendy.

> WENDY (CONT'D)
> I'm so sorry. That belongs to my father.

Unclear what Wendy is referring to, the woman looks at her with a quizzical expression.

> WENDY (CONT'D)
> (nice, but loud)
> The pillow!

The woman now looks concerned. Maybe even quietly panicked.

> WENDY (CONT'D)
> It doesn't belong to you. It belongs to my father.

Wendy tries to pull the pillow from the Old Lady, but she won't release her grip.

> WENDY (CONT'D)
> Please let go. It doesn't belong to you.

Wendy pulls again and this time succeeds in removing it from the old woman's hands.

> WENDY (CONT'D)
> Thank you.

Then, a bellowing, unearthly MOAN.

> OLD WOMAN
> Nooooh!

Wendy, terrified, pivots around into a CLOSE UP and the CAMERA TRACKS with her as she walks down the corridor toward her father's room. In the background, an ATTENDANT hurries over to comfort the woman.

> ATTENDANT
> Mrs. Friedman, what happened, honey?

Wendy flinches at the sound of the attendant's voice, but like someone escaping from the scene of a crime, she does not look back.

129   **INT. LENNY'S ROOM - CONTINUOUS**   129

Wendy enters and hands the pillow to Lenny.

                              WENDY
                    Here you go, Dad.

He pushes it away.

                              WENDY (CONT'D)
                    Dad I thought you might like this to prop
                    yourself up. Here, lean forward.

She sandwiches the pillow between her father's back and
the headboard.

                              WENDY (CONT'D)
                    There.

She stands back to observe her caretaking accomplishment,
but Lenny wiggles the pillow out from behind his back and
pushes it away. It lands on the floor.

                              WENDY (CONT'D)
                    Dad.

She picks up the pillow and brushes it off.

                              JON
                    Wendy, forget it.

                              LENNY
                    I don't wannit.

                              WENDY
                    Are you sure? I think you'd be more
                    comfortable.

Again, she tries to prop it behind Lenny.

                              LENNY
                         (sharp)
                    I don't want it! Can't ya hear?!

Lenny violently pushes the pillow back at Wendy. Wendy
just stands there with it, humiliated and stunned.

                              LENNY (CONT'D)
                         (to Jon)
                    What the hell does she think I'm payin'
                    her for, to bother me?

Wendy's eyes immediately well up. Jon sees this.

                              JON
                    Wendy, he doesn't know what he's talking
                    about.

She throws the pillow on the floor, picks up the cat carrier and rushes out of the room in tears.

130   **EXT. NURSING HOME PARKING LOT - NIGHT**   130

The door opens and Wendy stumbles out, holding her cat carrier. She wipes her nose with the top of her hand and then just stands there leaning against the wall and sniffling.

Slowly she turns to her left to discover that she is not alone out there.

Leaning against the wall a few feet away is a GROUP OF STAFFERS on a break, among them, Jimmy, who smokes a cigarette and nods to her.

Wendy produces a weak smile, then turns back to stare at her shoes. She's wearing a pair of unattractive flats with thick socks. She hates what she sees.

                    JIMMY
          You want one?

Wendy looks up to see Jimmy offering her a cigarette. She shrugs in the affirmative. Jimmy slides over and hands her one.

                    WENDY
          Thanks.

                    JIMMY
               (lighting it for her)
          Nobody smokes anymore, right? We're
          stupid to smoke. Especially after
          spending time here and still doing it,
          that makes us extra stupid.

Wendy smiles politely and takes a drag.

                    JIMMY (CONT'D)
          What's in the box?

                    WENDY
          My cat.

                    JIMMY
          Takin' it out for a walk?

Wendy smiles a little. There is a long awkward silence as Jimmy and Wendy stand there smoking among the frozen cars. Genghis MEOWS from the Carrier.

                              JIMMY (CONT'D)
          Your cat is cold.

                              WENDY
          Yeah.

                              JIMMY
          You want to sit in my van? I'll turn on
          the heat.

                              WENDY
          No, it's okay. I'm going to go back in
          in a minute.

They stand there for another moment. Jimmy sees Wendy
shiver a little.

                              JIMMY
          C'mon. This is nuts. I'm right over here.

Jimmy chivalrously picks up the cat carrier and ushers
Wendy over to --

HIS BEAT UP VAN

He opens the passenger side door and quickly clears off
the seat by tossing some of the junk into the back. He
helps Wendy in and hands her the cat carrier.

131   **INT. VAN - NIGHT - CONTINUOUS**   131

He gets in on the driver's side and immediately TURNS THE
IGNITION and THE HEAT. He digs around and offers a
crushed box of Kleenex to a snotty Wendy. She accepts.

                              JIMMY
              This place is crazy, right?

Wendy lets out a quick breath of air in agreement. Jimmy
takes a drag from his cigarette. They sit there. It's
too intimate.

                              JIMMY (CONT'D)
                    (looking inside carrier)
              You mind if I introduce myself?

Jimmy opens the little metal door and takes the cat out.

                              JIMMY (CONT'D)
          What's his name?

                    WENDY
          Genghis. As in Genghis Khan. It's a
          she.

Jimmy plays expertly with the cat. He immediately makes
her purr.

                    JIMMY
          She's a lover, not a fighter. Yes she
          is. How's he doing?

Wendy looks at him.

                    JIMMY (CONT'D)
          My friend in B-26.

                    WENDY
          He's good. Well, I mean, you know, not
          good, but fine. Okay.

                    JIMMY
          He likes Tater-tots.

Wendy looks at him. Huh?

                    JIMMY (CONT'D)
          It's the only thing he touches sometimes.
          I slip him extras when I can. Double
          serving.

Wendy smiles.

                    JIMMY (CONT'D)
          You married?

                    WENDY
          No... but my boyfriend is.

Jimmy laughs.

                    JIMMY
          Does your mother know you're doing that?

                    WENDY
          She's not really in the picture.

                    JIMMY
          She dead? That's why she never comes
          around?

                    WENDY
          No, just kind of obsolete in the parent
          department. She was never very good at
          it. Neither was my father actually.

                         JIMMY
          So that's why a pretty woman doesn't have
          a husband and a family of her own.

Wendy blushes at the attention.

                         JIMMY (CONT'D)
          What do you do when you're not here?

                         WENDY
          Oh, stuff.

                         JIMMY
          I mean, I'm an aide in a nursing home,
          what are you?

                         WENDY
          Oh, I'm...a...a theater person. I mean,
          I temp too, for money...but that's not my
          main thing. I write plays.

                         JIMMY
          Like Shakespeare?

                         WENDY
          Yeah, well, not as good.

                         JIMMY
          What're yours about?

                         WENDY
          My plays?

                         JIMMY
          Can I read one?

                         WENDY
          Are you kidding?

                         JIMMY
          No.

                         WENDY
          You actually want to read one of my plays?

                         JIMMY
          What's so strange about that?

                         WENDY
          In my world nobody really wants to read
          somebody's unproduced play.
                    (off Jimmy's look)
          I just printed out a copy of the draft
          I'm working on. I've got it in my bag.

                         JIMMY
          Great. I've got a long shift. I'm doing
          graveyard.
                    (awkward silence, then --)
          Your father is doing okay, by the way.
          He's got some time left.

                         WENDY
          How do you know?

                         JIMMY
          I keep an eye on him. I noticed.

                         WENDY
          Noticed what?

                         JIMMY
          His toes. They haven't started to curl
          under yet.
                    (off Wendy's look)
          The toes curl under a few days before
          they go.

                         WENDY
          Is that like a Jamaican folklore thing or
          something?

                         JIMMY
          It's something I learned from being here.
          We all talk about it. It's always the
          same.

                         WENDY
          The toes curl?

                         JIMMY
                    (nodding)
          Like the witch in "The Wizard of Oz." A
          couple of days before.

                         WENDY
          Why, do you think?

                         JIMMY
          They say it's the air leaving the body.

A strange silence. Then Jimmy blows a smoke ring. It
floats in the air. They both stare at it.

                         JIMMY (CONT'D)
          I'm from Nigeria, by the way.

132   **INT. LENNY'S ROOM - NIGHT**   132

Lenny is asleep. The bed is in the upright position. It suddenly begins to HUM as it is lowered by Jimmy.

Wendy quietly sets up SMALL BOWLS for Genghis's food and water. Genghis sits on top of the red pillow.

Wendy pulls A COPY OF HER PLAY from her bag and hands it to Jimmy.

CLOSE ON THE TITLE PAGE --
"Wake Me When It's Over," a play by Wendy Savage.

Jimmy smiles. Wendy smiles back. Jimmy quietly heads out the door. They wave goodbye to each other. Once Jimmy leaves, Wendy goes to the end of the bed and gently lifts the sheet.

HER POV OF LENNY'S FEET --
a little crooked from a lifetime of use, but basically intact.

               JON (OS)
         (whispering)
    Wendy.

Wendy turns to see her brother waiting for her outside the door with his coat on. He lifts up his hands to say, "what're you doing?" She covers Lenny's feet, shuts off a light and tip toes out of the room. The lava lamp glows.

                      FADE TO BLACK.

UNDER BLACK --
THE SICKENING SOUND OF CHEERY SLEIGH BELLS.

                      FADE IN:

133   **INT. NURSING HOME HALLWAY - DAY**   133

A LARGE CHRISTMAS TREE is being carried down the hall. The person who carries it is totally obscured by the bulk of the branches. It looks like the tree is walking by itself.

               SONG
     Just hear those sleigh bells jingle-ing
     Ring ting tingle-ing too,
     Come on, it's lovely weather for a sleigh
     ride together with you....

134   **OMITTED**   134

135   **EXT. MALL PARKING LOT - DAY**   135

It's decorated for Christmas. Over a P.A. system the
song continues to play --

> SONG
> Giddy-yap giddy-yap giddy-yap let's go
> Let's look at the snow
> We're riding in a wonderland of snow...

Lenny has a shopping bag on his lap as Jon pushes him
toward the car. Wendy also carries shopping bags.

AT THE CAR --

Lenny is already inside. With Wendy's help, Jon places
the folded-up wheelchair into the trunk. As Jon closes
the trunk, Wendy goes to open the door on the driver's
side but she can't.

> WENDY
> Jon, it's locked.

Jon stands there for a moment looking at Wendy over the
roof of the car. He has something on his mind.

> WENDY (CONT'D)
> C'mon Jon. Open it.

> JON
> They published the list in the paper and
> your name wasn't on it.

> WENDY
> What?

> JON
> The Guggenheim Foundation took out an ad
> in the New York Times announcing their
> fellows for the year and your name wasn't
> on it.

> WENDY
> That's weird. I guess it was an
> oversight. Can we get in? I'm freezing.

> JON
> It wasn't.

                    WENDY
          What?

                    JON
          An oversight.

                    WENDY
          How do you know?

                    JON
          Because I called the Guggenheim
          Foundation.

                    WENDY
               (through clenched teeth)
          Will you let me in the car.

Jon unlocks the door.

137   **INT. JON'S CAR - CONTINUOUS**   137

Wendy angrily pushes the driver's seat forward and climbs
past it into the backseat.

                    WENDY
          Hi Dad.

                    LENNY
          Hi.

Jon gets in but doesn't start the car. He's not letting
this go.

                    JON
          I called them to find out why your name
          wasn't on the list.

                    WENDY
          Why would you do that?

                    JON
          I was looking out for you.

                    WENDY
          You were policing me. You're sick.
          That's sick, Jon.

Jon starts the car and puts it into REVERSE.

                    JON
          You're the sick one, Wendy --

He backs out of the parking space and in his agitated state almost hits a FAMILY OF SHOPPERS.

THROUGH THE REAR WINDOW -- the FATHER of the family BANGS his open palm on the trunk.

> FATHER
> Hey! Idiot! Look where you're going.

138   **INT./EXT. JON'S CAR - HIGHWAY - DAY**   138

Jon drives, glancing in the rear view mirror at Wendy, who sits arms crossed. Lenny wearily endures the ride.

> JON
> A friend of mine does some consulting for
> The Guggenheim Foundation and he looked
> you up in the computer. You've been
> rejected eight times.

> WENDY
> So -- how many times have you been
> rejected?

> JON
> That's not the point. Six.

> WENDY
> The point is that you don't think I have
> any talent. The point is that you called
> them because you just couldn't believe
> your little sister was good enough to get
> one of them.

Sick of the bickering, Lenny pulls his wool hat low and sinks into his seat. His HAND drifts up to his ear.

ECU LENNY'S EAR --
as his trembling finger reaches behind it and PUSHES THE SWITCH on the HEARING AID. All SOUND DROPS into an AURAL MUTED HAZE.

A small expression of relief comes over Lenny's face as he drifts into what looks like a state of content resignation. His eyelids get heavy. He looks at Jon and Wendy. They continue to argue, but THE WORDS ARE MURKY. They might be saying something like this:

> JON
> That's not true.

                    WENDY
          Yes, it is. You wanted your suspicions
          confirmed. You're just like him. He
          never thought I was good at anything
          either.

Lenny leans his head against the window and looks out.

HIS POV --
of the highway passing by. It's all slightly blurry and
dreamy.

139   **EXT. THE VALLEY VIEW - DUSK**   139

The Corolla pulls into a parking space. Jon climbs out,
then Wendy. Jon opens the trunk, hoists the wheelchair
out and sets it on the ground.

                    JON
          Where did the money come from, Wen?

                    WENDY
          I got a grant.

                    JON
          Cut the crap, Wendy.

Jon SLAMS the trunk shut.

                    WENDY
          I got a grant, Jon! I did! Okay, fine,
          I didn't win a Guggenheim. Big fucking
          deal. It was a different kind of grant.

                    JON
          What kind?

                    WENDY
          What?

                    JON
          You said you got a different kind of
          grant. What did you get?

An agonized pause from Wendy. She squirms around and
then finally surrenders.

                    WENDY
                (weakly)
          Feema.

                    JON
          What? I've never heard of that.

                         WENDY
                    (repeating flatly)
          Feema.

                         JON
                    (to himself, confused)
          Feema? Feema...
                    (getting it)
          FEMA. Federal Emergency Management?

Wendy nods her head yes.

                         JON (CONT'D)
          You took money from FEMA...

                         WENDY
          I was granted the money.

                         JON
          What was the federal emergency?

                         WENDY
          Nine-eleven.

                         JON
          What's that got to do with you?

                         WENDY
          I work downtown. I was affected.

                         JON
          Everyone was affected. The whole world
          was affected. But they're not going
          around taking money away from people who
          really need it.

                         WENDY
          There was no work for months. All the
          temps applied. I didn't do it at
          first... Look, I'm trying to get my life
          together.

                         JON
          By stealing money from the federal
          government?

                         WENDY
          I didn't steal it, Jon. There was a
          thing where you could apply if you lost
          twenty-five percent of your income or
          something like that. I can't remember the
          details. Call FEMA. Ask them.
          Apparently they care about me more than
          you do.

Wendy grabs the wheelchair and rolls it around to the
passenger side of the car. She swings the car door open.
Inside, Lenny sits with his eyes closed.

140   **INT. NURSING HOME - NIGHT**   140

CLOSE ON THE LAVA LAMP glowing. CLOSE ON LENNY in bed
staring at it.

The CAMERA drifts down the side of his body which is
covered in a white sheet and finally stops at the bottom
of his bed where his feet pointing upright create a TENT.

After a moment, the tent begins to cave in. His toes are
curling under. Genghis sits on the windowsill staring at
him. She MEOWS, then jumps down and runs out of the room.

                                            FADE TO BLACK.

UNDER BLACK --
RING! RING! RING!

140A   140A

141   **INT. JON'S BEDROOM - NIGHT**   141

A PHONE IS RINGING. Jon asleep in bed reaches for it.

                    JON
              Hello?... Yes... It's okay, what's
              wrong? Is he alright?...

Jon snaps on a light and sits up. Wendy appears in the
doorway and drifts into the room.

                    JON (CONT'D)
              What?... Really? When? Okay. I
              understand. We'll be right over.

Jon hangs up the phone.

                    WENDY
              Is he okay?

                    JON
              It's not Dad. It's Genghis.

Wendy stares at Jon.

                    JON (CONT'D)
          She got in a fight with that other cat.
          They want us to get her now.

Wendy rushes to get ready. Jon lumbers out of bed,
irritated.

                    JON (CONT'D)
                    (yelling O.S.)
          I told you that cat was a bad idea!

142   **INT. NURSING HOME - NIGHT**   142

A SECURITY GUARD leads Wendy down a hall to a CLOSED DOOR
with a small window. He opens the door for her.

143   **INT. FAMILY SITTING ROOM - NIGHT - CONTINUOUS**   143

Wendy enters to find Jimmy on his knees looking under A
COUCH. The room is designed for coziness. There are TWO
STUFFED CHAIRS, AN AREA RUG and a FAKE FIREPLACE.

                    WENDY
          Hi.

                    JIMMY
          Hi. She's under here. She won't come out.

Wendy bends down beside Jimmy, they both look under the
couch at Genghis who stares back at them.

                    WENDY
          What happened?

                    JIMMY
          I don't know. They were getting along
          fine before.

                    WENDY
          She's totally freaked out.

                    JIMMY
          You should see Winston.

                    WENDY
                    (trying to coax Genghis out)
          C'mere bunny. C'mon, it's okay. C'mere.
                    (to Jimmy)
          Sometimes if you just ignore her, she comes.

Wendy and Jimmy pull their heads out from under the couch
and sit on the floor next to each other.

Jimmy crawls over to the nearby FAKE FIREPLACE and
SWITCHES IT ON. The logs glow red.

Jimmy returns to his place beside Wendy. They stare at the
illuminated rotating lights inside the plastic logs.

                    JIMMY
I read your play.

                    WENDY
You did?

                    JIMMY
Uh huh. I liked it.

                    WENDY
No way, really? You didn't think it was
a bunch of middle-class whining?

                    JIMMY
No.

                    WENDY
I was scared that you'd think that I was
just some spoiled American brat moaning
about her difficult childhood.

                    JIMMY
Not at all. I thought it was sad.

                    WENDY
But you're from Haiti.

Wendy's odd comment lands there. Jimmy raises his
eyebrows and looks at her with amusement.

                    WENDY (CONT'D)
That's probably a really hard place to be
from.

                    JIMMY
Yeah, but my parents didn't scream at
each other or hit each other or scream at
us. They weren't... What do you call it
in the play?

                    WENDY
Pathologically narcissistic.

                    JIMMY
Right. They weren't crazy people. It
sounds like your family wasn't very good.

The bluntness of Jimmy's observation hits Wendy. Her
throat suddenly tightens.

                    WENDY
          It wasn't.
                    (choking up)
          It. Was. Bad.

Unable to control herself, she begins to cry.

                    WENDY (CONT'D)
          I'm sorry.

                    JIMMY
          It's okay.

She lowers her head, covers her face with her hands and sobs.

                    WENDY
          Oh god, what's my problem? I'm always
          crying in front of you.

                    JIMMY
          It's good to cry.

Jimmy puts an arm around Wendy to comfort her. After a
moment of this, Wendy raises her head and looks at him.
He smiles warmly. And then, overwhelmed by his kindness,
Wendy lunges toward him and kisses him on the lips, he
kisses back and then gently pulls away.

                    JIMMY (CONT'D)
          I should probably get back to work.

                    WENDY
          Oh, okay. Um... I'm sorry.

                    JIMMY
          Don't be sorry.

                    WENDY
          I thought that...um...you were being so
          nice...that I...
                    (suddenly writhing)
          Oh god, I'm so gross.

                    JIMMY
          No. You're great...you're funny and I
          like your play...

Wendy stops writhing and looks at Jimmy and smiles.

                    JIMMY (CONT'D)
          It's just that... I'm in love with my
          girlfriend. That probably sounds like corn.

Wendy is shot in the heart, but tries to rally herself.

                        WENDY
            Corny. No. It's great. I'm really
            happy for you...

And with that, Wendy bursts into tears. Jimmy puts his
arm around her. Genghis crawls out from under the couch.

                        JIMMY
            Look who it is.

144   **EXT. VALLEY VIEW - NIGHT**   144

The Corolla is parked out front, with Jon asleep at the
wheel. Wendy exits the nursing home, holding Genghis.
Jimmy walks beside her and carries the LARGE HOODED
LITTER box. She opens the door and climbs in.

INSIDE CAR --

Wendy pulls the door shut. Jon comes to and looks at Genghis.

                        WENDY
            Pop the trunk.

                        JON
            Huh?

                        WENDY
            The trunk.

Jon groggily twists around to see --

JIMMY, through the rear window, holding the BIG HOODED
LITTER BOX.

The trunk lid pops open, momentarily hiding Jimmy. And then
it's slammed shut and Jimmy reappears. He waves. Wendy
waves back as the car pulls away.

145   **INT. JON'S HOUSE - LIVING ROOM - DAY**   145

Wendy sits on the windowsill with her beat up LAP-TOP
typing. Genghis is nearby, exploring her new
surroundings. An album PLAYS.

146   **INT. COLLEGE CLASSROOM - DAY**   146

His back to a room full of undergrads, Jon writes on a
chalkboard where he has drawn some sort of chart.
"Dramatic Theater" is written on one side and "Epic
Theater" on the other.

>   JON
>   (pointing to the chart)
>   Here there is <u>emotion</u>, an interest in
>   what people are <u>feeling</u>. Whereas Brecht
>   wants people to <u>think</u>.

Jon crosses out the word "emotion" and underlines the
word "thinking" over and over again.

>   JON (CONT'D)
>   In "Dramatic Theater" we have <u>suggestion</u>,
>   but Brecht wants an <u>argument</u>.

BEEP. BEEEP. BEEEP. Jon's cellphone rings. He pulls
it out and looks at the caller id.

>   JON (CONT'D)
>   (to class)
>   Excuse me for one minute.

Jon turns his back to the class and mumbles into the
phone. His students watch him. After a few moments, Jon
clicks the phone shut and just stands there with his back
to the room.

>   STUDENT
>   Mr. Savage?

Jon turns around. He seems dazed.

>   JON
>   Yes?

>   STUDENT
>   What's the difference between "plot" and
>   "narrative?"

Jon looks bewildered.

>   STUDENT (CONT'D)
>   You wrote it on the board.

He glances over his shoulder to the chalkboard and sees
that he has written the words "Narrative" and "Plot" in
opposite categories.

>   JON
>   Oh. Uh. That's a good question.

>   STUDENT
>   They're both just story, right?

Jon is stumped and distracted. He just stands there,
unable to form any more words.

147   **INT. JON'S HOUSE - LIVING ROOM - DAY**   147

Wendy still sits on the windowsill typing. The phone
begins to RING. She gets up, walks out of FRAME and
answers it.

                          WENDY (O.S.)
              Hello?

148   **INT. BUFFALO HOSPITAL HALLWAY - DAY**   148

Wendy and Jon walk quickly toward the NURSES STATION.

149   **INT. HOSPITAL ROOM - DAY/NIGHT**   149

Wendy and Jon enter to find --

LENNY IN A HOSPITAL BED--
his eyes closed, an IV in his arm. He doesn't look good.
Monitors beep.

Wendy and Jon just stand there looking.

LATER --

It's NIGHT NOW. Wendy and Jon are camped out in chairs
facing Lenny.

                          WENDY
              Do you want some coffee?

Wendy looks over at Jon and realizes he's asleep. She
stands and approaches Lenny, reaching out to touch his
hand.

                          WENDY (CONT'D)
              Jon?

                          JON
                     (groggy)
              What?

Jon looks at Wendy first, then at Lenny. He rises from
his chair and goes to stand next to his sister. They
stare at Lenny in silence. He's dead.

                          WENDY
              That's it?

                          JON
              Yeah.

A long still pause.

151   **INT. NURSES STATION - NIGHT**   151

A HOSPITAL NURSE sits behind the desk writing a report.

                          WENDY (OS)
               Excuse me?

The nurse looks up to see Wendy looking hollow and spent
and Jon, behind her in his coat, shivering.

152   **INT. HOSPITAL HALL - NIGHT**   152

From behind we see the Hospital Nurse walking briskly
down the hall toward Lenny's room. Her rubber soled
shoes squeak.

153   **INT. HOSPITAL ROOM - NIGHT**   153

The privacy curtain is pulled around the bed. Lenny's
clothes and things are put in a plastic bag by the nurse.

154   **EXT. HOSPITAL - DAWN**   154

Wendy and Jon stumble out of the hospital onto the empty
streets. Wendy carries the plastic bag with Lenny's clothes.

155   **INT./EXT. CAR - DAWN**   155

POV FROM CAR of the empty city of Buffalo passing by.

Jon sits in the passenger seat looking out the window.
He turns to his left to SEE --

WENDY BEHIND THE WHEEL --

Jon watches her for a long time as she drives. He's
struck by this vision of his little sister as a capable
person, as if seeing her for the first time.

                          JON
               You're not a bad driver.

Wendy looks at him with a tiny smile.

                          WENDY
               Really?

                              JON
                Really.

156   **INT. HOUSE - MORNING**   156

        HIGH ANGLE of Jon and Wendy asleep in their clothes on
        Jon's bed. Genghis sleeps beside them.

                                              FADE OUT.

157   **INT. LENNY'S ROOM/HALL/LOUNGE - LATE AFTERNOON**   157

        Wendy and Jon pack up Lenny's belongings. Wendy empties
        drawers. Jon hoists the T.V. and VCR off the bureau and
        heads for the door.

                              JON
                I'll be right back.

                              WENDY
                Okay.

        Wendy listlessly sits on the side of the bed, clearing
        off the night stand, when she comes upon LENNY'S GLASSES.
        She picks them up and puts them on. They are over-sized
        and odd looking on her, and her eyes are hugely
        magnified. She goes to the mirror over the dresser and
        looks at herself.

        Suddenly, something catches her attention. She removes the
        glasses and looks up in the air, listening to the music
        wafting down the hall. It's a slow RHYTHM track. Then, the
        ETHEREAL SOUND OF A FEMALE VOICE begins singing "The Look of
        Love." Wendy drifts out of the room into --

        THE HALL --

        No one seems to be around. The halls are empty. She walks
        towards the sound of the music and finds herself outside.

        THE LOUNGE --
        where an entertainment is occurring, crowded with
        residents and staff.

        WENDY'S OBSTRUCTED POV -
        of a MALE and FEMALE musical act.

        Wendy turns to discover a METAL STAND with A BLACK AND
        WHITE publicity shot of "Burt & Lizzie," the same act she
        and Jon saw singing in the Best Western Oasis Room. They
        finish the song and the audience applauds.

> LIZZIE
> Thank you. Thank you. I'm Lizzie --

> BURT
> And I'm Burt.

> LIZZIE
> And we're thrilled to be here at the
> Valley View. We're in town for a week
> playing the Roof Room at the Hyatt and
> decided to come here because this place
> has special meaning for Burt and me.
> Burt's mother was a resident here, Nettie
> Adelson and well, this is for her.

Lizzie launches into a soulful rendition of "Weeping
Willow Tree." It plays over the following scenes --

160   **INT. HALLWAY**   160

Jon and Wendy walk down the hall carrying an odd
assortment of Lenny's belongings and some boxes.

161   **OMITTED**   161

162   **INT. TRAIN - DAY**   162

The urban outskirts of Buffalo rush by. Wendy sits and
looks out the window.

                                          DISSOLVE TO:

163   **INT./EXT. CAB - NIGHT**   163

The sights heading downtown on Second Avenue blur by.
Wendy sits in the back of the cab looking out the window.

164   **INT. WENDY'S APARTMENT - NIGHT**   164

Wendy is unpacking. She sets up the Lava Lamp on her
bureau, turns it on and stares at it.

THE SOUND OF LIGHT KNOCKING. Wendy goes to the door and
opens it a little ways. On the other side is Larry.

> LARRY
> Hi.

                    WENDY
          Hi.

                    LARRY
          I saw you come in.

Wendy sees that Larry is holding some flowers.

                    LARRY (CONT'D)
          These are for you.

                    WENDY
          Thanks.

She takes them and brings them to her nose to smell them.

                    LARRY
          They don't have a scent. They're from
          the deli. I never understand why that is
          with flowers from there. I guess you
          have to go to a real florist and pay
          extra if you want the nice smell.

Wendy smiles and stands there. It's awkward.

                    LARRY (CONT'D)
          Can I come in a minute?

Wendy opens the door and Larry enters.

                    WENDY
          Where's Marley?

Larry immediately mists up.

                    LARRY
          I wasn't going to tell you about it. I
          mean, it must seem ridiculous compared to
          what you've been going through. You had
          a human being die on you --

                    WENDY
               (soft and sad)
          Oh no.

                    LARRY
          A significant human being. Your father.

                    WENDY
          He's dead?

                    LARRY
          We're going to do it tomorrow.

Wendy looks at him, upset.

                    LARRY (CONT'D)
          His legs. He can't get around anymore. He
          can't get up on the bed. He's so depressed.

                    WENDY
          He's always been kind of mopey.

                    LARRY
          It's not the same. She stopped eating.
          There's a surgery, but the vet says
          there's no guarantees. And the
          rehabilitation is brutal. She's old,
          Wen. She's in pain.

Larry breaks down crying. Wendy tries to comfort him. They
hug. Larry tries to kiss her, but she doesn't kiss him
back. Her arms hang limply by her side. When he realizes
he can't inspire her lust, he stops and steps back.

                    LARRY (CONT'D)
          I'm sorry about your Dad.

                    WENDY
          I'm sorry about Marley.

                    LARRY
          If you ever want to re-indulge in
          unhealthy compromising behavior, you know
          who to call, right?

Wendy smiles. Larry steps outside the door, walks down
the hall and heads for the stairs. Wendy stands at the
door, watching him go. After a moment --

                    WENDY
          Larry...

He turns back.

                    WENDY (CONT'D)
          Can I ask you something?

Larry looks at Wendy, hope brimming in his eyes.

                    WENDY (CONT'D)
          Not about us, about Marley...

                                        FADE TO BLACK.

FADE IN:

165   **INT. KITCHEN SET - DAY (LATE 1960'S DECOR)**   165

GRAINY BLACK AND WHITE IMAGES OF THE THREE STOOGES
slapping each other around.

A YOUNG BOY, sits on a counter between two cabinets as
his FATHER yells at him and smacks him.

The Boy doesn't react to the slaps, instead he looks over
his father's shoulder to a small TV playing THE THREE
STOOGES. Larry, Curly and Joe are going at it. The
CHAOTIC SOUNDTRACK is amplified. As the father continues
the beating, the boy magically BEGINS TO FLOAT UP IN THE
AIR. *What is this we're watching?* A memory? A dream?
The boy drifts up and hovers above his father. After a
moment, the father "breaks character," shades his eyes
and speaks to someone offscreen.

                    FATHER
          Do I react once he goes up?

ANOTHER ANGLE reveals that we are in --

A THEATER

The kitchen is a set in a little downtown space. The boy
and the father are actors in a play. We are witnessing
some kind of TECHNICAL REHEARSAL.

A LIGHTING DESIGNER is programming cues. Wendy is there in
the nearly empty house. She, responds not to the actor on
stage, but to the DIRECTOR who is seated beside her.

                    WENDY
          No. He doesn't know it's happening.
          It's a manifestation of the boy's
          internal state.

                    DIRECTOR
          Uh huh.
               (calling out to the stage)
          Paul, just keep up the beating like the
          boy is still there...

ON STAGE --
The father pummels the now empty space where the boy had
once sat. The lights on stage go out so now the only
thing visible is the boy, suspended in mid-air.

IN THE AUDIENCE --
Wendy speaks over her shoulder to someone behind her.

                         WENDY
              Do you think it's too much?

REVERSE ANGLE reveals --

JON --
He's been watching the rehearsal and despite his best
efforts to control himself, his face is streaked with
tears. He wipes them away with his fingers as he speaks.

                         JON
              No. The, uh, naturalism with the
              magic-realism... together. It's, uh,
              effective.

Wendy twists her head around.

                         WENDY
              Are you crying?

                         JON
              No... I'm... I'm... impressed.

Wendy smiles.

166   **EXT. THEATER - NIGHT**   166

Jon and Wendy walk toward an avenue. Jon has a suitcase.

                         WENDY
              Thanks for coming.

                         JON
              Thanks for inviting me. I'll see the
              real thing when I come back through.

                         WENDY
              Okay.

Jon raises a hand to flag a cab.

                         WENDY (CONT'D)
              Do you hate me for using stuff from your
              life in the play?

Jon thinks about it and then shakes his head no.

                         WENDY (CONT'D)
              You don't think it's self-indulgent and
              bourgeois?

                         JON
              It's good, Wendy.

A cab pulls up, Jon opens the door. They hug awkwardly.

                    JON (CONT'D)
          Wish me luck on my paper.

                    WENDY
          What's it called?

                    JON
          "No Laughing Matter: Black Comedy in the
          Plays of Bertolt Brecht."

Wendy smiles and nods. Jon becomes insecure.

                    JON (CONT'D)
          Bad title?

                    WENDY
          No, it's good. I like it. Where's the
          conference?

                    JON
          Poland.

Wendy's jaw drops open.

                    WENDY
          You didn't tell me that.

                    JON
          You didn't ask.

Jon smiles and shrugs as he climbs into the cab.

                    WENDY
          You're going to Krakow?

                    JON
          Warsaw. Then Krakow...

Wendy grins widely.

                    JON (CONT'D)
          We're just gonna check in... play it by
          ear. You know, see how we feel about
          each other... as people.

Wendy and Jon smile at each other, amused by his familiar habit
of emotional back-peddling. They kiss goodbye. The cab takes
off. Wendy watches it go.

167   **INT. WENDY'S APARTMENT - EARLY MORNING**   167

ON THE T.V. an exercise program plays. Wendy follows along.
Suddenly fed-up with the inane instructor, she snaps it off.

168   **EXT. EAST RIVER PARK - DAY**   168

Wendy jogs along the East River Esplanade. The CAMERA
TRACKS alongside her. It's still early in the morning and
the sun is rising over Brooklyn. The water glistens. In
the cold air we see and hear her breath as she goes.
Wendy is not an experienced runner, but she's giving it a
try. She runs for a while and then turns around, so now
she's JOGGING BACKWARDS. She calls to someone who is O.S.

                          WENDY
                  (breathless, cheerful)
            Come on, honey! Come on! Let's go!

She turns back around so now she's running forward again.

A LOW TRACKING SHOT --
of WENDY'S CONVERSE SNEAKERS slapping the cement. The
CAMERA SLOWS a little and Wendy's feet run out of frame.
Now, just the vertical posts of the iron fence pass by
and then we hear the SOUND OF PANTING GETTING CLOSER as --

MARLEY ENTERS THE FRAME. Her lame hind legs are affixed
to a WHEELCHAIR CONTRAPTION -- a cart with pneumatic
wheels that ROLL behind her -- but this doesn't deter her
from her favorite outdoor activity.

The CAMERA TRACKS alongside Marley as she defies all
expectations and runs gloriously forward. Her front legs
pump vigorously. The sun flares behind her.

We stay with her for an extended amount of time -- a full
minute -- or until the FLASH FRAME appears and the FILM
ROLLS OUT of the camera.

                                           CUT TO BLACK.

                    THE END

CAST AND CREW CREDITS

FOX SEARCHLIGHT PICTURES
in association with
LONE STAR FILM GROUP
presents

THE SAVAGES

LAURA LINNEY PHILIP SEYMOUR HOFFMAN PHILIP BOSCO PETER FRIEDMAN GBENGA
AKINNAGBE CARA SEYMOUR DEBRA MONK DAVID ZAYAS and MARGO MARTINDALE

Written and Directed by TAMARA JENKINS	Executive Producers ANTHONY BREGMAN FRED WESTHEIMER	Co-Producer LORI KEITH DOUGLAS
Produced by TED HOPE ANNE CAREY	Director of Photography MOTT HUPFEL	Costume Designer DAVID ROBINSON
Produced by ERICA WESTHEIMER	Production Designer JANE ANN STEWART	Music by STEPHEN TRASK
Executive Producers ALEXANDER PAYNE JIM TAYLOR JIM BURKE	Film Editor BRIAN A. KATES, A.C.E.	Music Supervisor RANDALL POSTER Casting by JEANNE McCARTHY, C.S.A.

CAST

Wendy Savage . . . . . LAURA LINNEY
Jon Savage
. . . . PHILIP SEYMOUR HOFFMAN
Lenny Savage . . . . . . PHILIP BOSCO
Larry . . . . PETER FRIEDMAN
Eduardo . . . . DAVID ZAYAS
Jimmy . . . . . GBENGA AKINNAGBE
Kasia . . . . CARA SEYMOUR
Ms. Robinson . . . . . TONYE PATANO
Bill Lachman . . . . GUY BOYD
Nancy Lachman . . . . . DEBRA MONK
Doris Metzger . . ROSEMARY MURPHY
Burt . . . . HAL BLANKENSHIP
Lizzie . . . . JOAN JAFFE
Real Estate Agent . . . . LAURA PALMER
Mr. Sperry . . . . SALEM LUDWIG
Attendant . . . . SANDRA DALEY
Matt . . . . PETER FRECHETTE
Manicurist . . . . JENNIFER LIM
Nurse . . . . KRISTINE NIELSEN
Doctor . . . CHRISTOPHER DURHAM
Annie . . . . MADDIE CORMAN
Nurse #2 . . . . . . CYNTHIA DARLOW

Administrator . . . . . CARMEN ROMAN
Counselor . . . . . . NANCY LENEHAN
Resident #1 . . . . . MICHAEL HIGGINS
Resident #2 . . . . MADELINE LEE
Valley View Nurse . . . . TIJUANA RICKS
Roz . . . . . . MARGO MARTINDALE
Woman in Parking Lot . . . ERICA BERG
Howard . . . . . MICHAEL BLACKSON
Simone . . . . SIDNÉ ANDERSON
Woman with Red Pillow . . PATTI KARR
Father in Mall Lot . . . . JOHN BOLTON
Student . . . . ZOE KAZAN
Father . . . . LEE SELLARS
Director . . . . . . MARIANNE WEEMS
Valley View Nurse #2 . . . TOBIN TYLER
Physical Therapist . . . DEBBI FUHRMAN
Manicurist #2 . . . . LILI LIU
Boy . . . . . MAX JENKINS-GOETZ
Stunt Coordinator . . . . . MIKE RUSSO
Stunt Rigging . . . . ROY FARFEL
STEPHEN MANN
BRIAN SMYJ

CREW

Unit Production Manager
. . . . ROBIN NELSON SWEET
First Assistant Director . . CHIP SIGNORE
Second Assistant Directors . . . JESSE NYE
        ALFONSO TRINIDAD
Camera Operator . . . . PETER AGLIATA
1st Assistant Camera . . . . DAN HERSEY
2nd Assistant Camera/B Camera 1st Assistant
. . . . DAVID FLANIGAN
Camera Loader/B Camera 2nd Assistant
. . . . ELISA VASQUEZ
B Camera Loader. . . . . IAN CARMODY
Camera Department Intern
. . . . GIACOMO BELLETTI
Art Directors . . . SUTTIRAT LARLARB
        MARIO VENTENILLA
Set Decorator. . . . . CARRIE STEWART
Leadman . . . . JOSEPH F. PROSCIA
On Set Dresser . . . . . ANU SCHWARTZ
Set Dressers . . . . . . STEVE CATERELLI
        KARNIG PORYAZIAN
        KYLE SALVATORE
Art Department Coordinator
. . . . VANESSA MERRILL
Art Department Interns
. . . . ARIEL CHUDZIKIEWICZ
    MICHAEL ROSEBUSH-DICENZO
Production Sound Mixer
. . . . MATHEW PRICE, C.A.S.
Boom Operator
. . . . PAUL KORONKIEWICZ
Sound Utility . . . . JAN McLAUGHLIN
        TIMOTHIA SELLERS
Gaffer . . . . KEN SHIBATA
Best Boy Electric
. . . . . . LEIGHTON EDMONDSON
Electricians . . . . JOE CZERW,
        NINA KUHN, IRIS NG
Generator Operator
. . . . . . W. FRANK STUBBLEFIELD
Key Grip . . . . . . JIMMY MacMILLAN
Best Boy Grip . . . . DAVE McALLISTER
Dolly Grip . . . . DAN BEAMAN
Grips . . . . . . ANTHONY ARNAUD
        DIVINE COX
        STEVE PELEQUIN
Production Coordinator
. . . . MEGHAN K. WICKER
Assistant Production Coordinator
. . . . ALISON DAVIS
Production Secretary . . . PRITI TRIVEDI
Office Production Assistant
. . . . MICHAEL LIZZIO

Production Office Interns
. . . . ANTHONY CAUCHY,
NIKKI HUNG, ZACHARY KUCHNIKI,
MORGAN ROCHE, SHYLO SHANER
Post Production Supervisor
. . . . . . JONATHAN FERRANTELLI
Assistant Editor . . . . ALI MUNEY
Post Production Consultant
. . . . BRIAN McNULTY
Assistant Costume Designer
. . . . JOANNA BRETT
Wardrobe Supervisor . . . . . JILL GRAVES
Key Costumer
. . . . . . MEREDITH M. DRISCOLL
Wardrobe Assistant . . . . ADAM BUTERA
Wardrobe Interns . . JENNIFER CARNIVAL
        CASA WILSON
Production Accountant
. . . . ELIZABETH VERGHESE
1st Assistant Accountant
. . . . DANIEL WAGNER
Payroll Accountant . . CHANEL JACKSON
Payroll Services Provided by . . . . AXIUM
Key Make-up Artist . . STACEY PANEPINTO
Make-up Assistants . . CASANDRA KEATING
        DIONNE PITSIKOULIS
Key Hair Stylist . . . . . . JASON HAYES
Additional Hair Stylist
. . . . . . SHANNON HARRINGTON
Property Master. . . . . JEFF BUTCHER
1st Assistant Props . . OLENKA DENYSENKO
2nd Assistant Props . . . KLEY GILBUENA
Script Supervisor
. . . . MARIANA HELLMUND
Clearance Coordinator
. . . . GRACIE MENDELSOHN
Still Photographer . . ANDY SCHWARTZ
Special Effects Coordinator
. . . . JC BROTHERHOOD
Special Effects Assistant
. . . . MIKE MURPHY
Location Managers. . . . . . MIKE KING
        STEVEN WEISBERG
Assistant Location Managers
. . . . ERIC WROLSTAD
        KIMBERLY FEINMAN
Location Assistants . . ORIT GREENBERG
        OLIVER REFSON
        PRAGUE ROBERT
Location Scout . . . SASCHA SPRINGER
Locations Intern . . MITCHELL GUTMAN
Parking Coordinator . . . . . JOSE TEJADA
Second 2nd Assistant Director
. . . . NICHOLAS BELL

2nd Assistant Director—Buffalo
. . . . CHRISTOPHER CARROLL
Key Set Production Assistant
. . . . THOMAS GAITO
Set Production Assistants
. . . . JYOTA BERTRANG,
ANGELA CUTRONE, ANGELA HOW,
COREY "COMPLEX" ROBERTS,
KRYSTLE SOSA,
SALVATORE E. SUTERA
Assistant to Ms. Jenkins
. . . . MARK MIKUTOWICZ
Assistant to Mr. Hope
. . . . KARA BLANCHARD
Assistant to Ms. Carey
. . . . CLAIRE PACACHA
Assistant to Ms. Westheimer
. . . . JUSTINE COGAN
Assistant to Mr. Burke . . . ANNA MUSSO
Assistant to Mr. Bregman
. . . . STEFANIE AZPIAZU
24-Frame Playback . . . DENNIS GREEN
Casting Associate . . NICOLE ABELLERA
Casting Assistant . . MORGAN DONAHO
Extras Casting . . . . KAREN E. ETCOFF,
KEE CASTING
Extras Casting Associate . . BILL TRIPICIAN
Caterer . . . . GOURMET TO U
Chef . . . . ANTHONY TORRE
Craft Service . . . . . PATRICK BARILE
Craft Service Assistant . . . . RYAN BUA
Transportation Captain. . PETER CLORES
Transportation Co-Captain
. . . . DANNY BOY PAUSTIAN

New York Drivers

JIM LEMBO	JIM KELLY
GERARD MAGGIO	RICH MARINO
BOB JOHNSON	JOHN SINNOT
PAUL CASTIGLIONI	ED BATTISTA
MIKE O'BRIEN	HERB LIBERZ
RICH HUBKA	KEN JOHNSON
SCOTT ROTH	JOHN PALUMBO

Construction Coordinator
. . . . MARTIN BERNSTEIN
Construction Foreman. . MALCOLM REID
Key Construction Grip . . . SAM BURELL
Construction Grip . . . . GLENN BOWEN
Charge Scenic . . . . . ALAN J. LAWSON
Lead Scenic. . . . . . . STUART E. AULD
Camera Scenic. . . . . . . JESSE WALKER
Scenics . . . . BRUCE McNALLY,
CHRISTINE SKUBISH, DANIEL
CIAMPA, JESSICA NISSEN,
CATHY WASSYLENKO, NILI LERNER

Animals by . . . . . . STEVE McAULIFF
KIM KRAFSKY

Arizona Unit

Production Supervisor . . . . MIKE RYAN
Steadicam Operator. . . . . WILL ARNOT
2nd Assistant Camera. . . . . VON SCOTT
1st Assistant B Camera. . . . JOHN YIRAK
Set Decorator . . . . . MATT CALLAHAN
Set Dresser . . . . RICH FUENTES
Leadman . . . . SAM GUTIERREZ
Art Swing . . . . ROB PIERSON
Art Dept. Intern . . . TRACY SAGALOW
Production Sound Mixer . . NICK ALLEN
Boom Operator . . . . . . RON WRIGHT
Sound Utility. . . . . . DIANA CLELAND
Electricians . . . . MIKE AUFIERO,
JAMES BASTIAN, JEFF CLARK,
ERIK KOSKI, ROBERT McKAY,
GEOFF NANGLE, MICHAEL TESFAI,
JEREMY WREN
Dolly Grip . . . . GARY SHAW
Grips . . . . JAY COOLIDGE,
MIKE FREDERICKSON, SCOTT HESS,
TRAVIS HOLT HAMILTON, TRAVIS
QUEGAN
Production Office Coordinator
. . . . CONNIE HOY
Assistant Production Office Coordinator
. . . . . ANDREW PUTNAM-NELSON
Office Production Assistants
. . . . JOSH BLUTH
GARY PHILLIPS
Director/Producer Intern. . JILL LANDRITH
Production Interns . . . LISA ARBUCKLE
JULIE HOLMAN
Costumer. . . . . MAGGIE McFARLAND
Wardrobe Intern . . . . . JAMES BASTIAN
Make-up Assistant
. . . . LORETTA JAMES-DEMASI
Hair Assistant
. . . . . . CLAUDIA BRECKINRIDGE
Property Master . . . . CHRIS RUSSHON
Property Assistant . . . . . KEITH MOSCA
Props Intern . . . . JAYME SCHERE
Still Photographer . . . MARK FELLMAN
Location Managers . . ROBERT W. DAVIS
DENTON HANNA
Locations Intern
. . . . ANDREW GALLAGHER
Key Production Assistant
. . . . ERIK CARPENTER
Set Production Assistants
. . . . KATHRYN BOTKIN
JASON WOZNY

. . . . ROSEMARY GRAHAM
ROZE
Extras Casting . . . FAITH HIBBS-CLARK
Casting Intern . . . . KIT ABATE
Caterer. . . . CATERING EXCELLENCE
Transportation Coordinator
. . . . STEVE WAGNER

Buffalo Unit

Production Liaison . . . . . TIM CLARKE
Best Boy Grip . . . . . . RICK SEEBERG
Grip . . . . JOE BUNCE
Best Boy Electric. . . . . . . DAVE BULL
Electric . . . . BART DURKIN
2nd Assistant Camera
. . . . GERARD KAWCZYNSKI
Loader
. . . . KEVIN KILCHER
Assistant Props . . . . . . JON SCARDINO
Production Assistants
. . . . DAVE HARTER,
JUNE McCARTHY-DIMMING,
LAURA FELSCHOW,
NICK ADRIAN, RYAN DETZEL
Supervising Sound Editor . . BEN CHEAH
Assistant Sound Editor. . ERIC McALLISTER
Supervising Dialogue Editor
. . . . JACOB RIBICOFF
ADR Supervisor . . . . ANDREA HORTA
Foley Editor . . . . . . JOHN WERNER
Sound Effects Editor. . HEATHER GROSS
Foley Artist. . . . . MARKO COSTANZO
Foley Engineer . . . . GEORGE A. LARA
Foley Recorded at . . . . C5, INC
ADR Recorded at . . SOUND ONE, INC
SOUNDTRACKS, NEW YORK
WILSHIRE STAGES
Loop Group Coordinators
. . . . WENDY HOFFMAN
STEVE ALTERMAN
Re-recording Mixers . . . . DOMINICK
TAVELLA, ROBERT FERNANDEZ,
BEN CHEAH
Digital Scanning, Film Recording
and Digital Intermediate Services
. . . . LaserPacific A KODAK COMPANY
Digital Intermediate Timer. . DAVID COLE
Color Science. . . . . . . DOUG JAQUA
Digital Laboratory Project Managers
. . . . DONNIE CREIGHTON
RYAN HELSLEY
Digital Data Conform
. . . . VALANCE EISLEBEN
Digital VFX Supervisor
. . . . MICHAEL CASTILLO

Engineering Support
. . . . ANDREW GOODNEY
Music Editors
. . . . AMANDA GOODPASTER
JOSEPH BONN
Music Coordinator . . . . . JIM DUNBAR
Orchestrations by
. . . . DAMON INTRABARTOLO
Score Mixer. . . . . TIM O'HEIR
Score Recording Engineers
. . . . TIM O'HEIR
GREG HAYES
Assistant Engineer
. . . . PATRICIA FELICIANO
Post-Production Sound Facilities
. . . . SOUND ONE, INC
WIDGET POST
Negative Cutter
. . . . STAN SZTABA,
WORLD CINEVISION
Legal Services Provided by. . FRANKFURT,
KURNIT, KLEIN, & SELZ, PC
Insurance Provided by
. . . . DR REIFF & ASSOCIATES
Completion Bond. . FILM FINANCES, INC
Post-Production Accounting . . . JFA, INC.,
JOHN FINN, PETE HAYES
Post Production Interns
. . . . FRANZISKA BLATNER,
MATTHEW ENGLER, FIORELLA
GLAVE, JAMIE GROSS, SAM
KRETCHMAR, PETER SHANEL,
JASON SPENCER, STEPHANIE
DICHIARA, LOUISE FORD,
AMELIA GOLDEN, NED HARVEY,
SHARON PERLMAN, AARON
SHERMAN, DANIEL WARLOCK
Title Sequences Designed by
. . . . BIG FILM DESIGN
RANDY BALSMEYER
J. JOHN CORBETT
Dailies Telecine
. . . CREATIVE MEGA PLAYGROUND
Film Dailies
. . . . . TECHNICOLOR, NEW YORK
Cameras by . . . . ARRICAM
Camera and Lighting Equipment by
. . . . . . CAMERA SERVICE CENTER
Film Provided by . . . EASTMAN KODAK
Stage Facilities. . . SILVERCUP STUDIOS

About the Director/Screenwriter

Writer/director **Tamara Jenkins** began her film career writing and directing several award-winning short films, including *Family Remains,* which received a Special Jury Prize for Excellence in Short Filmmaking at the 1994 Sundance Film Festival. Jenkins' first feature film outing was 1998's *Slums of Beverly Hills,* which premiered as part of the Directors' Fortnight section of the Cannes Film Festival that year. Starring Alan Arkin, Natasha Lyonne, and Marisa Tomei, the film was nominated for two Independent Spirit Awards (Best First Feature and Best First Screenplay) and has since become a cult hit.

In addition to her feature film work, Jenkins' writing has been published in *Zoetrope: All-Story*, *Tin House Magazine*, and most recently her essay, "Holy Innocents," appeared in the book *Lisa Yuskavage: Small Paintings 1993–2004*, published by Abrams.

The Savages, Jenkins' second directorial feature film which she also wrote, had its world premiere at the 2007 Sundance Film Festival.